# THE BURDEN OF GRACE

IN THE CAROLYN ARCHER MYSTERY SERIES

Millicent: A Mystery
The Anastasia Connection
The Burden of Grace

ALSO BY VERONICA ROSS

Hannah B.
Homecoming
Fisherwoman
Order in the Universe
Dark Secrets
Goodbye Summer

# THE BURDEN OF GRACE

Veronica Ross

*A Midnight Original* MURDER MYSTERY

THE MERCURY PRESS

Copyright © 1997 by Veronica Ross

ALL RIGHTS RESERVED. No part of this book may be reproduced by any means without the prior written permission of the publisher, with the exception of brief passages in reviews. Any request for photocopying or other reprographic copying of any part of this book must be directed in writing to the Canadian Reprography Collective (CANCOPY).

The publisher gratefully acknowledges the financial assistance of the Canada Council for the Arts and the Ontario Arts Council.

AUTHOR'S ACKNOWLEDGEMENTS
The author wishes to thank the Ontario Arts Council for assistance.

Cover illustration: Photonica
Edited by Beverley Daurio
Cover design by Gordon Robertson
Composition and page design by TASK

Printed and bound in Canada by Metropole Litho
Printed on acid-free paper
First Edition
1 2 3 4 5 01 00 99 98 97

Canadian Cataloguing in Publication Data
Ross, Veronica
The burden of Grace
"A Midnight original murder mystery".
ISBN 1-55128-049-3
I. Title
PS8585.O842B87 1997    C813'.54    C97-92050-X
PR9199.3.R67B87 1997

The Mercury Press
2569 Dundas Street West
Toronto, Ontario
CANADA M6P 1X7

For Jay

# Chapter One

The first time I saw Gracie she was wearing crimson red lipstick and had a white Holiday Inn towel draped around her head. She was twelve years old and practising to be a nun. That was what the towel was for. The lipstick was, my grandmother said, because no one cared.

Gracie had read *The Nun's Story* and it was all she could talk about the summer my mother, Shirley, and her boyfriend, Reg, drove Gracie to Maine to stay with my grandmother and me. Reg was Gracie's father, which made us sort of step-sisters, although as Gram pointed out, Reg and Shirley were not married, and therefore the stress was on the "sort of." Gracie disagreed: Reg and Shirley were touring the midwest together in Reg's green Lincoln and if that didn't make us sisters, she didn't know what did. Shirley and Ray were staying in cabins where they would cook on hot-plates, or in motels where they would sit by the pool and drink cool pink drinks. They had their clothes in two suitcases, not one for him and one for her, but all jumbled up. So it was like they were married, and we were sisters. How much clearer could she make it?

Gracie was a chunky, strong girl with hazel eyes, skin that tanned, and long honey-blonde hair. Of course, the hair would have to go, she informed me as she brushed it. They would shave it off in the convent, but no one would ever see her bald head, not even the other nuns, because at night you wore a cap on your head.

She sighed dramatically telling me this. She knew exactly how it would be, she said.

"I'll be in love with this guy, see, and he'll really really love me, but he'll know I have to be a nun. He'll give me a single red rose on the day I go in, and once a month he'll come and stand by the gates of the convent when the moon is out."

"But how will you know?" I watched her brushing and brushing that golden hair and thought that if someone were to shave my head I'd kill myself. I was a twig compared to Gracie and my brown hair tended to frizz in the damp Maine weather. But even so. "How will you know he's out there, if you're locked in your cell?"

"I'll just know, that's all. He won't get married to anyone else or anything like that."

"Wouldn't you feel like sneaking out to see him?"

"No, I'd just lie there and suffer."

Gracie wasn't even Catholic. She wasn't anything, although she accompanied Gram and me to the Presbyterian church once in a while when Gram felt like going. Gram wasn't much of a church-goer, and she found the whole nun business tiresome. And the prayer business, because Gracie prayed long and hard before meals: "Please God, we thank you most holy for this wonderful meal of fish chowder and the biscuits dear Gram has so kindly made with her own hands. And please, oh heavenly Father, would you make Gram more understanding if we want to hang around Campbell's Drugstore for soda pop? There really isn't anything wrong with girls hanging around the drugstore, especially if one of the girls is used to the big city and is more sophisticated."

Gram would interrupt before the amen.

"I think God's heard enough, Gracie."

"But I haven't explained yet, and I want to tell Him to take good care of my father and Shirley!"

By the end of the summer, Gram was mumbling a brief prayer herself before we ate so that Gracie would not have a chance to start her conversation with God.

But I think Gram ended up liking Gracie, who was always cheerful, helpful, hard-working— and talking about the nunnery as she scrubbed the kitchen floor. Gram would come downstairs in the morning and find Gracie (in her bathing suit at first; Gracie wore one of two bathing suits constantly, as an outer garment if the weather was warm enough, or as underwear, until Gram figured out that Gracie simply did not own any underwear) on her knees with the scrub brush. Or Gracie might have the cupboard beneath the kitchen sink cleaned out, or the windows washed. In the week before she left, Gracie even painted the back porch.

I don't think this was because Gracie felt she had to pay her way. Being dumped off by her father, who was going on a trip with a woman he had only met a month before, seemed as natural for Gracie as calling his employer when he was hung over or doing the laundry in the bathtub.

Reg was a salesman, and one of the reasons for the midwest trip was to peddle encyclopedias door-to-door, town-to-town.

Gracie's mother had left with a guy she met in the bar where she worked, Gracie informed me cheerfully. She did not see this as at all strange, as many of the townspeople did, that my mother had left me at Gram's when I was five years old. It was supposed to be for a few months, but there I was, at twelve, still there.

"See, our mothers both ran off and that makes us even more like sisters," Gracie said. She lit my cigarette. We had to bend our heads down out of the wind because we were at the shore. At least no one would see us there, I thought. I'd wanted to stand watch outside the drugstore while Gracie bought the Camels, but she insisted I walk along the street and whistle. Me standing watch would make it seem like she was robbing the place, she said.

Smoking was okay, she said. She sneaked Reg's smokes all the time. He didn't care. But she'd have to give up cigarettes when she went into the convent. She thought the man who really really loved her would smoke when he stood outside the nunnery walls at the full moon. Was there anything more romantic than a heartsick man smoking? she asked me.

"Maybe our parents will get married while they're gone," I suggested.

"Nah." She blew smoke into the air. "Dad's still married to my mother. He can't find her to divorce her."

"Maybe your mother will be in one of the towns they visit."

"Better not be! Her boyfriend said he'd shoot Dad dead! But we're still sisters, okay?"

"Okay."

I really wanted to be her sister then. But at the end of August, Reg drove to Maine alone to pick up his daughter. He and my mother had split, he said philosophically as he dug into a slice of Gram's blueberry pie.


I didn't see Gracie again for years and years.

My new murder mystery, *Murder at the B & B*, brought our reunion about. My other mysteries were set in pioneer Canada— I'd moved to Canada with my first husband in the seventies— but the bed-and-breakfast novel was contemporary, peopled with rich tourists, an actor from California, a New York socialite and even an English lord. Suddenly Carolyn Archer was a household name. I went on tour with my book, appeared on *Good Morning*

*America* and other talk shows. Fan mail arrived from people asking when they could expect my next mystery, where they could buy my earlier books, and if the bed-and-breakfast place really existed. There were so many letters, including notes from a few crazies, that my thirteen-year-old nephew, who was visiting us that summer, helped to stuff envelopes.

"I didn't know you had a sister." Matthew gave me a strange look as he passed me the letter.

"Must be a crazy. Let's see." Three men had proposed marriage to me in the fan mail. A woman in New Jersey insisted she was my reincarnated grandmother. And at least eight people were praying for my salvation.

Those letters all had something weird about them: drawings of hearts, references to scripture, money for return postage (and my reincarnated Grandma had sent me a photo and a clipping about an automobile accident she had been in), but this letter Matthew handed me was done with a laser printer on good paper.

It was, of course, from Gracie. She had seen me on *Good Morning America* and she had read my book. Did I remember her? She had warm memories of my grandmother and of me, although Maine, "where I lived in my bathing suit and taught you to smoke," seemed a million years ago. She lived in Chicago and worked as a teacher in a private school. She would be delighted to hear from me.

She'd signed it: *Fondly, Your "sister" Gracie.*

"The quotation marks mean she knows she isn't really my sister," I told Matthew, after I explained a bit about that summer with Gracie so long ago.

"Gee, I didn't notice them." He blushed. "I would have known what she meant if I'd noticed them. Are you going to get in touch with her?"

"I don't know yet. I'll think about it."

I thought about it for three weeks. My life was fine now; very fine, in fact. I was happily married to Peter Hall, who owned The Bookworm, a bookstore in downtown Guelph, a small city in southern Ontario. I had friends, my writing. All the changes in my life, including a sad, traumatic first marriage, always made the past seem murky, not to be re-visited. I still owned my grandmother's house in Maine, but I hadn't been back there in years, although I had promised Matthew a trip.

In the end, curiosity overcame me. What *had* happened to Gracie, with the white towel on her head and her bright lips? She had seemed so unusual at the time, but when I thought of her at all, which was seldom, I was sure her life had turned out to be a disaster: marriage at seventeen, babies, drunken husband, several common-law relationships, more kids, trailer city somewhere.

But here was this literate, charming letter. A teacher— Gracie? How had this happened, with her father bringing her up in his topsy-turvy world? I thought of Reg's sleek moustache, his skinny neck and dirty shirt collar.

I learned about Gracie's transformation in the first of many long telephone conversations. Reg had abandoned her the year following her hiatus in Maine. It wasn't real abandonment, he hadn't meant it; he just got drunk and sort of forgot about her, but he disappeared for two weeks and the school authorities had contacted Child Welfare, who placed Gracie in a foster home.

"A former priest, would you believe it?" she asked in her throaty, rich voice. "He left to get married and they decided to take in foster children. I was the first and they ended up adopting me. I was fourteen years old by then!"

We told each other everything in the months that followed. She learned about my first marriage and I heard about a long-term relationship she'd had with a married man. I told her about meeting Peter, The Bookworm, Peter's wonderful mother, Marion, who was like a mother to me. I let my Labrador retriever, Conrad, bark into the phone to Gracie. I confided to her that the bed-and-breakfast in my book had been based entirely on the one Peter's parents owned in the north.

We would be going up to Meredith at Christmas, I told her, and on impulse, invited her to spend the holidays with us. I immediately regretted this: Christmas was a family time. How did I know if Gracie would fit in? Would I even still like her when we actually met face to face again?

Gracie accepted at once.

And being the Gracie I remembered, she did not ask if my in-laws would mind.

Marion and Hugh did not mind. They had room now that they'd put the addition on to their big brick house.

But Peter minded. He can be a curmudgeon sometimes.

"Meredith and Ho-Ho together are bad enough, but this Gracie person sounds pushy to me," he said as we drove north. "I wish we were staying at home. Just the three of us."

"Conrad'll get to run in the free north, like a real Labrador retriever." Conrad woofed at the sound of his name. "Anyway, Christmas is a time to be charitable."

"Christmas is a time to spend money." He peered at the road. Light snow was falling.

"Oh, shut up. You like Christmas, but just won't admit it."

"We don't even get a chance to look her over first. If she'd flown to Toronto, we could have put her back on the plane if she was a monster."

"She won't be a monster. She sounded fine on the phone. Interesting and lively."

"I don't have a good feeling about this."

"She's flying into Sault Ste. Marie to save us having to pick her up at the Toronto airport. And if we'd driven her up, she'd have had to sit in the back with Conrad. She'd have been covered in yellow dog hair by the time we got to Meredith. Plus, he'd try to sit on her lap. How would you like to drive two hundred miles with a hundred-pound dog on your lap?"

"Maybe she weighs three hundred pounds," Peter said hopefully, but a little more cheerfully. Discussing his beloved Conrad always did this to him. "She didn't send a picture."

"I didn't either. We just talked on the phone. I'll kill you if you're not nice to her."

"I'm always nice. Always polite, that's me."

That was true, I thought, but looking at his frowning face, I wished he didn't have that peaky look he gets in the winter. A shrunken look. With his glasses and thinning blonde hair, he looked so conservative, so nerdy. It was ridiculous, but I wondered what Gracie would think of him.

I would soon find out.

My father-in-law, Hugh Hall, retired Police Chief, English expatriate and owner of the Meredith Bed-and-Breakfast, had always been a chauvinist of the first order. For years, Marion had had dinner on the table at six, then washed up afterwards while Hugh, spent from tackling speeders, game poachers and town drunks, and from kibbitzing with village businessmen over coffee in the Ritz Cafe, dozed on the couch. Clean shirts and socks found their way miraculously to his dresser drawers. Hugh was hungry? Tea and scones appeared, served on a tray.

Things had changed somewhat in recent years, but there was always a time when Hugh took over the kitchen, and that was at Christmas. Goose or turkey, plum pudding or mincemeat pie: these were momentous questions, ultimately decided by Hugh. I had picked up Christmas crackers and chutney for the feast in response to Hugh's telephone orders. Except for the bird, he didn't actually cook the meal, but it was very much his production, and he oversaw the preparation of potatoes and Brussel sprouts, salad and condiments, the heating of plates and the cooling of the wine.

This year the fowl of choice was goose, I knew. Marion had lamented to me that Hugh planned to put the bird right on the oven rack, with a dripping pan on a lower rack. Once upon a time, cleaning the oven after this greasy procedure would have been Marion's job, but Hugh had been warned that he would have to wash out the oven.

Not even Hilary, the girl they had hired during the tourist season, and who would be joining us for Christmas, was to do Hugh's dirty work, Marion insisted.

Hugh wasn't worried by any of this when he threw open the door. Snow was coming down heavily by then and a fire burned in the grate. I'm always cheered by Hugh and Marion's house, by its brick solidity, so rare in the north; by the wide verandah, now garlanded with pine wreaths and bows. A large fir tree stood in the bay window and a delicious smell, shortbread, I guessed, filled the air.

Hugh carried a glass of port, which was almost upset by Conrad as he raced into the house to find Marion.

"Damn dog," Hugh muttered, but his eyes were shining; he'd probably been sipping all afternoon, I thought. "It comes from not working the fellow. We'll have to do something about that."

"You're not taking Conrad hunting," Peter insisted as Hugh kissed me. Conrad was barking in the kitchen, ordering Marion to feed him treats.

"It'll be the making of him. Steven and I are going."

Steven MacLeod, a young doctor from Scotland, had recently opened a practice in Meredith. He was also courting Peter's sister, Allison, who had gone back to school to be a nurse.

"Well, you'll have to go without Conrad," Peter said. "Conrad! Come here!"

"You're not turning into one of those animal rights nuts, are you?" Hugh asked, as Conrad, followed by Marion, darted from the kitchen. Conrad had cookie crumbs around his muzzle, but he was doing his darnedest to lick them off.

"Oh, do be quiet, Hugh," Marion said. She kissed me. "Go unload the car," she told Hugh. "Give Peter a hand. How are you?" she asked me. "We were worried about the driving. Hugh even called the Department of Highways."

As always, I was amazed. Marion kept getting younger and younger looking. First the grey hair had gone, replaced by auburn, and now it was a soft, more natural brown. The handmade sweaters had been switched to sporty polyester, which was then traded for ethnic sweaters and cotton blouses. Today, Marion wore an Indian beaded necklace, an oversized cotton shirt, and jeans. Only the frilly apron reminded me of the old Marion.

"Come into the kitchen, Carolyn. You can probably use a cup of tea. And come and meet your friend."

But the friend was standing in the doorway. Gracie. Gracie? She was beautiful. Still a bit heavy, but her hair was long and the honey-blonde colour I remembered. It framed a pert but strong face that was perfectly made up. She wore a green jumpsuit and gold jewellery, bangles and chain necklaces, and dangling earrings with green stones that matched her outfit.

She gave me a sultry, amused smile.

"I caught an earlier plane because of the storm forecast," said that rich voice I had heard so often in recent months.

Perfume wafted over me as we embraced. She felt big and solid. I was still a twig compared to her. And then I sneezed. Perfume always did that to me.

Gracie had arrived that morning, by taxi, from Sault Ste. Marie. With the north so sparsely settled, it is not unusual for people to drive two hundred miles to, say, a hockey game or to go shopping, but taxis are something else. Someone coming off a drunk might hire a taxi for a hundred-mile ride home, but— a taxi from the Soo!

Gracie shrugged. She would have rented a car, she said, but she wasn't familiar with the roads. And she didn't want to trouble Hugh or Marion. A taxi seemed the simplest thing. Anyway, she was on holiday. And:

"What's money for if not to spend?" she asked, as Marion poured my tea.

"We would have come for you," Marion said. "Or Allison could have driven to the Soo in that van of hers."

Allison had taken her share of the sale of the house after her divorce and bought a van.

"Well, perhaps Allison can drive me back to the airport in that van, then." Gracie watched as Marion put cookies on a plate. She had brought a dried-flower arrangement for Marion, followed by delivery from a florist in North Bay of a gigantic poinsettia and a dozen red roses. It had taken the taxi driver two trips to the front door to carry her luggage and Christmas presents into the house. She had presented Hugh with a large bottle of Crown Royal whiskey. I hoped she hadn't bought me an expensive present. I had picked out silver jewellery for her from Peru and a book about Canada. I knew Marion had made Gracie thrum mittens and a matching one-size-fits-all hat.

"Tea, Peter?" Marion asked, pouring it before he could answer.

"Maybe Peter would rather have some whiskey, after that long drive," Gracie suggested.

"We can open Hugh's Crown Royal," Marion said.

But Gracie had other ideas. She had a bottle for Peter, too. It was still packed in her luggage, but she'd get it, she said.

"She's kind of overwhelming, isn't she?" Peter asked after Gracie had left the room.

"Well, she doesn't weigh three hundred pounds," I said, "so you were wrong about that. I hope the visit works out. I really should have checked with you, Marion, before I invited her."

"Anyone who brings me a bottle of Crown Royal can't be all bad," Peter conceded, helping himself to a cookie.

"Nonsense," Marion told me. "It was perfectly all right. We could use a change."

"I thought you'd had enough changes lately," Peter said. Marion and Hugh had had a busy fall, not only putting up hunters from the States, but German tourists as well.

"And she won't be the only newcomer," Marion went on. "Steven will be joining us as well for Christmas. And Hilary, of course."

Gracie's laughter, followed by a squeal, came from the hall.

"Absolutely wonderful!" Gracie cried, laughing as she came

into the kitchen, carrying the whiskey and a sprig of plastic mistletoe.

"I caught your husband," she told Marion. Hugh, red-faced and bemused, stood in the doorway. "I know it's silly, and I tried to get the real McCoy, but plastic had to do."

She grinned at Peter: should she kiss him, too? He bit into another cookie and lowered his face. Marion got up to fetch glasses.

"Your husband's a shy one," Gracie told me.

## Chapter Two

Shopping for stocking fillers in Meredith has always been a tradition. The Guelph stores and boutiques stock much more interesting doodads and baubles, but Christmas wouldn't be Christmas without Marion and I making a trip to the Metropolitan with its creaking wooden floor and narrow aisles, and to Roan's Drugstore with the dusty Evening in Paris cologne and loofah bath mitts in ancient plastic bags.

Meredith comes into its own at Christmas. The snow is piled almost waist high. There's something magical about the tinkling of the bell as you enter Roan's, about the bundled children and the green and red garlands in the Metropolitan. The large tree in front of the post office is decorated with lights beside a manger scene. The decorations are tackier than those in southern Ontario, but this small town tackiness is cosy, familiar. "Good morning, Marion. Merry Christmas!" "Oh, hi, Carolyn. Nice to see you again. Merry Christmas!" The nosiness and gossip seem transformed to heartiness and caring at Christmas time.

In the Metropolitan I picked up bath salts for Peter (a joke), socks that looked hand-knit but were, in fact, made in Hong Kong, a tiny china Conrad (ditto for Hugh), a plastic change purse with a maple leaf flag on it, and a pair of red boxer shorts with Santa's face on the seat. Miniature cars for Allison's kids, including a Rolls Royce for Matthew. Lifesavers, mints, pencils, erasers, pencil sharpeners, fridge magnets, crayons; recipe cards for Marion (who pretended not to see as I sneaked to the cash register) and handkerchiefs; and a trashy novel about a hooker and a cop for Hugh. Jokey make-up and ear muffs for Allison.

I bought Gracie a change purse, soap, a folding drying rack for over the shower, a teacup with roses and "Meredith" printed on it, and a notebook with hockey players on the cover.

There was another tradition, too: the purchase of a nightgown for myself. Every year I bought myself a flannelette nightgown in the dime store. The Meredith Nightshirt, Peter called it. It was always pastel, flowered, and probably cheaper in Guelph, but I looked forward to purchasing that new nightie.

And then I ducked into The Lady's Style Shoppe to choose another gift for Gracie. Going by what she had already presented, the gifts I had chosen seemed paltry.

The trouble was there was nothing among the acrylic sweaters and subdued dresses that I could imagine Gracie wearing, and we headed down the street to Meredith's one and only craft boutique, where I found a large glazed brown bowl and a matching pitcher. While that was being wrapped, I chose a pewter letter opener made in Nova Scotia. It had a lobster etched in it, just the thing to remind Gracie of Maine, I thought.

Gracie and I had stayed up late the night before my Meredith shopping trip, discussing Maine and my grandmother. It amazed me that she remembered details I had completely forgotten. Had we really broken Gram's best china platter and hidden the pieces? I had a vague memory of that platter, which had an English cottage scene on it, but I couldn't recall breaking it. And I did not remember that we both tried on my grandmother's corset. On the other hand, Gracie did not remember painting the porch.

"It's so long ago," she agreed. "But you don't know how much I envied you, living with your grandmother in that wonderful house. All summer I had this half-wish that Reg would not return. At the same time, I was afraid he'd leave me there, and then where would I be? If you can understand that. I think Reg is the reason I never married. I came close several times, but I always held back."

I asked her if she'd ever seen Reg again.

"He turned up out of the blue when I was at university," she said ruefully. "Don't ask how he found me. He wanted to borrow money, said he'd give anything to be family again."

"I bet you lent him the money."

"Gave him the money is more like it, because I never heard from him again except for a phone call the next year when he was drunk and feeling sorry for himself because Christmas was coming.

"Actually, you know, he caused me a lot of trouble. In my mind, I mean. I was in therapy for years. I'm pretty sure he molested me."

"That's awful."

"I just remember bits. You don't know how lucky you were to grow up with your grandmother who didn't have any horny boyfriends around. What about your mother?"

"She died years ago. I visited her the year after you were in Maine. It wasn't the greatest experience."

I usually didn't like talking about my mother and I hardly ever thought of that disastrous trip to Chicago after my mother, who still had legal custody, had threatened Gram with court if I didn't visit. The trouble was, by the time I arrived, my mother had a new boyfriend in the picture, and after three weeks she packed me off to Gram again.

"And then you had that rotten marriage," Gracie prompted. "To that Charlie."

"And then I had that rotten marriage. Thank goodness that's over and done with."

"Never hear from the bastard?"

"I think he's dead. He disappeared and they never found the body. That's what I heard, anyway." The truth was that Charlie had disappeared after he contacted me years later, but that was one story I didn't want to think about. I had been trying to find out the truth about a friend who had died and who had claimed to have been secretly married to Edward VIII. "It's awful to say, but I'm only relieved not to have heard from him again."

"I'm glad you're happily married now," she said.

"Even though Peter's shy? I know he's not the most out-going person."

"If you love him, that's all that counts," Gracie said. "It doesn't matter what anyone else thinks."

"Well, I do love him."

"Never tempted?" Gracie raised an eyebrow.

Was I tempted? I had met many interesting men during my book tour, and there was nothing like being a star, however temporary, to add allure to a woman. There had been hints, passes, suggestions, but I had ploughed ahead with the grinding schedule of the book tour.

Gracie seemed to read my mind.

"You must have come across all kinds of fascinating male creatures during all the hoopla around the book."

"Oh, sure. But if it hadn't been for the book none of them would have looked twice at me. I mean, I'm not that interesting a person or that gorgeous. And I was too tired. Book signings all day, a late dinner, and an eight o'clock plane to catch the next morning." Suddenly I thought of Neil Andersen, an Ontario Provincial Police officer with whom we had become close. I liked Neil's friendly, laid-back manner, his ease. Although Neil was a cop, he took a lighter look at things than Peter generally did. Neil was divorced. He enjoyed my cooking and I often made the dishes he liked...

"If I ever fool around," I giggled, "it wouldn't be with some Romeo I only met once. The only man I'd possibly consider would be this guy, Neil. Not that I would. Have an affair, I mean."

I had actually gone on to tell her all about Neil, who did seem pretty attractive at 2:00 a.m.

It was wine talk, silly talk, much like Gracie's chatter about the lover and the convent.

But not entirely meaningless talk. I knew as soon as I said the words that I was attracted to Neil. Sometimes he dropped in for a coffee afternoons when Peter was at the store. Neil's friendly interest in my writing had grown into something more personal. We could talk for hours about people, childhood, influences. I had never consciously thought: wouldn't it be wonderful to have an affair with Neil? But when the doorbell rang and Neil stood there, I was happy. We always found something to discuss.

There was a chemistry between us, and saying the words had made it seem very real.

When we were finished shopping, Marion and I had lunch, as we did every year, at the Ritz Cafe. We always had the same thing: club house sandwiches and coffee in thick white mugs. As usual, the bacon was burned. And as always, people kept coming out of the kitchen at the back where they'd obviously imbibed. It was Christmas Eve afternoon, after all.

"I wonder if I shouldn't have pressed Gracie to come along with us today," I said, after the waitress (the same one as last year), refilled our mugs. "I know she said she'd cook dinner, but maybe she really wanted to come."

"I don't think so. She seemed quite happy to stay behind with the men for company," Marion laughed.

"Peter was going to sleep anyway and then wrap my presents. He always leaves that to the last minute. But what about dinner? Do you mind?"

Marion shrugged. "She seems to want to show off her culinary skills. Let her cook. I won't have to."

"She was that way in Maine too. Scrubbing floors, washing windows, you name it. I guess she hasn't changed much. My grandmother would come downstairs in the morning and there Gracie would be, hard at work. All this doing so much must come from insecurity. She has the most wonderful memories of Maine. She remembers things I've completely forgotten. Trying on my grandmother's corset, for instance. I remember the two of us looking at it while Gram had her bath, but I didn't remember actually trying it on." I shook my head.

"English cousins of mine reminded me of things, too. Stealing apples— I had completely forgotten. And locking another cousin in the lavatory. I just hope Hugh doesn't go through too much of that whiskey. His snoring sounded like thunder last night."

"Peter said Gracie's perfume gives him a headache. It makes me sneeze."

"Men get foolish as they get older," Marion said. "You should have seen Hugh with one of the German women. She looked like a model. Her husband had a migraine and she stayed up talking to Hugh until two in the morning. They went through a large bottle of red wine. He was distracted for a day or two after she left."

Marion looked amused.

"You don't think Gracie will try to get her hooks into Hugh?" I blurted. "I mean she's so overpowering that it would be so obvious, so blatant. It would be funny!"

"Exactly," Marion said.


Allison's van was in the driveway when we returned at two-thirty. Allison had recently moved to North Bay, half an hour's drive away. I hadn't seen her since the summer, when she was in the middle of moving. The house had been sold; her divorce to Joe was final. After buying the van, there was just enough to cover rent on a townhouse in North Bay and day-to-day living expenses until she graduated with her R.N.

She met Steven MacLeod in September, when he arrived in Meredith and moved into Marion and Hugh's bed-and-breakfast, where he remained until he found a place of his own. I hadn't met Steven because we'd gone to Montreal for a short vacation at Thanksgiving instead of coming up north, but according to

Marion, the attraction between the young Scottish doctor and Peter's younger sister had been immediate. There was even talk of marriage: Allison would work with Steven after she graduated.

This situation was hard for me to grasp. I had never known Allison when she wasn't with huntin' and fishin' Joe. She and her boys had stayed with us in Guelph for a while until she returned to Joe. But she had gone back with old ambitions rekindled. Joe had been against the nursing training, but Allison had forged ahead.

Still, I couldn't picture beer-drinking, smoking-like-a-chimney Allison married to a doctor. Unless he liked the down- to-earth, plain-spoken type, which Allison certainly was.

As I stepped out of Marion's car, I saw Matthew's head peering through the curtains of the front door. He soon disappeared— he was fourteen now, "cool"— but I knew he'd be grinning, waiting for me.

"So you bought out Meredith," he said, seizing parcels. I slapped his fingers away and grinned back.

"Big galoot," I said, resisting the temptation to ruffle his hair, which I was glad to see had grown in. He'd had it shaved to his scalp in the summer. I set my bags on the floor and poked him in the ribs. "It's no good peeking. Your real gifts are hidden away."

His brothers, Timmy and Jody, rushed in then and stared at the bags before accepting hugs. The television was on in the living room.

"Where's your mother?" Marion asked. I knew Allison had to deliver the boys to Joe at four. Joe would have them until ten, but they'd have Christmas morning here. "And where's Grampa?"

Matthew said everyone was in the kitchen with Gracie.

Peter, too?

Peter too.

"They're drinking whiskey!" Jody cried.

They might all have known one another forever, I thought. Peter, Hugh, Allison and Gracie were sitting around Marion's round table, the whiskey bottle set in the middle. Allison was smoking. I could tell from Peter's flushed face that he'd had quite a bit to drink. He grinned at me foolishly.

"So I don't see why I have to deliver the kids to him. Not after the way he's been harassing me," Allison was saying. "Calling and hanging up. Calling and hanging up."

She'd had her hair cut. The short frizzy perm of reddish curls that had looked so bizarre around her angular face was gone, as was the heavy make-up she'd used to stamp herself as a new, liberated woman. You could see her freckles again. She looked years younger, almost like a teenager, in her jeans and sweatshirt with a wolf on it. I noticed she wore a small gold locket on a chain— a gift from Dr. Steve?

"How do you know it's Joe?" Peter asked. "Could be anyone."

"Can you find a chair?" he asked me.

"Boys have to see their dad," Hugh said.

"I would feel exactly the same way you do," Gracie told Allison. Gracie looked wonderful in jeans and a loose, flowing green and navy striped t-shirt. Her hair was tied back at the nape with a scarf.

She smiled at me and poured me a drink.

"Christmas Eve," she said. "You might as well live dangerously."

A spicy smell filled the kitchen. I wondered what was in the oven. The big goose sat thawing on the counter.

"Hugh and I made the stuffing together," Gracie informed me. "It's all done and the salad's in the refrigerator. There's nothing else to do except to enjoy the wonderful company." She passed me a glass filled with about three inches of whiskey and one of ginger ale.

"I will drive the kids," Hugh said, just as Marion entered the kitchen.

"Not if you've been drinking," Marion said, eyeing the level in the whiskey bottle. "That would be all we need, you caught for drunken driving as you're delivering the boys to Joe."

Hugh made a face, but he put his glass down.

"And I don't particularly want Joe here, after what happened at Thanksgiving." Marion plugged in the tea kettle.

"Divorce," Gracie sighed, looking sympathetically at Allison.

"What happened at Thanksgiving?" I asked Marion.

Allison answered. "Mr. Gross-out turned up and threatened to beat up Steven. It was disgusting. And I'm not taking the boys over. I don't care. Someone else can take them if you're all so keen on them going over to his old mother's place. I don't think they even want to go."

"They'll want the presents," Marion said. "I'll take them, then, if you won't. Let's not have any fuss, Allison. The boys have got to go and that is all there is to it."

"Steven says he wants to adopt the boys," Allison told Gracie, which led to the story of Gracie's own adoption by that wonderful couple.

I had to hand it to her: Gracie could tell a good story, and she didn't hesitate to tell on herself. She had stolen from the couple at first; she had even taken the wife's engagement ring, just to wear, and then lost it! She sneaked drinks from the liquor cabinet, hooked off school, and had a wild party when they were out.

"So how did this young hooligan turn into a law-abiding citizen?" Hugh asked.

"Knitting," Gracie said, smiling at Marion. "My foster mother's mother arrived for a visit and taught me to knit. She reminded me of your grandmother," she told me, "and I knew I had to cut the high-jinks out. Nan taught me to knit. At first I wanted to impress her, because I knew my mom had told her about all the awful things I'd done. I wanted to prove my mom wrong, I guess. Maybe even make her out to be a liar! So Nan started me out with a sweater, just straight knitting, and I guess I wanted to prove to everyone that I wasn't so awful. By the time that sweater was done, I was different.

"I kept thinking of you, Carolyn, and your grandmother. With Nan it was just like you and your grandmother.

"When Nan got sick with cancer, I went to Arkansas to stay with her. We were always close. Of course, by then I still wasn't the sainted angel I had pretended to become. I used to sneak outside for a smoke when Nan was napping, and oh, my goodness, I fell in love with the garbage man, of all people. Smart guy, should have gone to university, but lacked the money, and the ambition, too. Tony. Luckily, Nan slept a lot. Tony and I drank beer on the swing at night."

"Sneaky, I'd say," Hugh laughed.

"You have to do what you have to do," Gracie retorted with a grin.

"What happened to this Tony?" Allison wanted to know.

"Oh, Nan died and I returned to Chicago. Sanity restored. It was a very hot summer."

"In more ways than one, I bet," Hugh said. Peter laughed.

"I didn't know you were a knitter," Marion said.

"Not lately. You're the knitter, from what I hear," Gracie told her. "Maybe you can get me started again."

"But that's enough about me." Gracie turned to Allison. "Tell me about your wonderful Scottish doctor."

I was surprised to see Allison blush. She twirled the locket.

"I met him when he was staying here with Mom and Dad. One thing led to another, I guess. I said I was through with men, but there he was."

"And never married?"

"He helped to get his brother and sister educated. He had girlfriends, but none who wanted to play second-fiddle to his family."

"He took to the boys right away," Marion said. "It would have been impossible otherwise."

"Is he good-looking?" Gracie wanted to know. "I bet his accent gets to you. Danny Boy and all that. But that's Irish, I think."

Allison blushed again. Steven wasn't bad-looking, she said.

"Stick compared to Joe, but there you go," Hugh said undiplomatically. "Those Scots lads can be tough, though."

"Well, I think it's wonderful he would care about his siblings that much," Gracie said. "I guess after they were educated he wanted to strike out for himself."

"He always wanted to see Canada," Allison said. "He had a chance to work in Toronto, but he said that wasn't the Canada he'd pictured. And then he came to Meredith."

"Good old Meredith," Peter said, "the land of timber wolves and bears. And snow." He winked at me.

"Not everyone's a city slicker," Allison protested. "I lived down south for a while, but I guess I'll stick to the north," she told Gracie. "People are friendlier up here, even in North Bay. Steven says we'll move to North Bay if that's what I want."

"Better not," Hugh said. "We need a doctor right here."

"I gather Steven's made a hit, then," Gracie said.

"He's very popular," Marion said. "Even makes house-calls to the elderly, and that is rare today. He takes his time with his patients, too. A few of the fellows we've had here just filled in time until they could move elsewhere. Steven is just the kind of old-fashioned doctor we need. We're lucky to have him."

"I can't wait to meet him," Gracie said. "Your wonderful Steven," she told Allison.


I went with Marion to deliver the boys to Joe, whose mother lived on the outskirts of Meredith. Gladdie's house was like so many rural places, a basic clapboard bungalow with pieces added on over the years. There was a woodpile to the side, and a rusty car sat on blocks in the rear of the house. But a plastic wreath hung on the front door and Christmas lights were strung around the windows and door. Smoke was coming from the chimney and with the snow the scene looked cosy.

A white curtain lifted as we pulled into the yard and Gladdie's pointed face peered out. I had met Gladdie many times at Allison and Joe's, but I didn't know how friendly she'd be. She'd taken Joe's side in the divorce, which was natural, but Marion had told me that Gladdie was spreading the most awful talk about Allison and her "fancy Limey doctor" around Meredith.

The boys, especially Matthew, hung back at first— divided loyalties?— even when their father, big and husky behind his frail mother, appeared at the door. Matthew busied himself gathering the gifts for Joe and Gladdie.

"Go on, then," Marion said, and at last Jody and Timmy rushed to their father, who swooped them up. Gladdie took the presents from Matthew.

"It's just not fair Joe can't have the boys for Christmas morning," she told Marion. "She has them the rest of the time."

"I try to keep out of it," Marion murmured.

"I guess she didn't want to show her face around here," Gladdie said. "And that's another thing. The boys get to see their relatives on her side more than Joe's people."

"Be quiet, Ma." Joe set Timmy down. His mother gave him a dark look and went into the house.

"Someone'll be back for the boys at ten," Marion told Joe. "And Merry Christmas."

"Yeah, sure. You, too."

"He seems to have accepted the situation," I told Marion on the way back. "Better than I would have thought."

"I suppose he had no choice. There was never much wrong with Joe. He just wasn't for Allison. But his old mother's a different kettle of fish. The fact that Allison has a doctor boyfriend is something that really bothers her, doctors in these parts being considered next to God Himself."

"When is Steven coming?"

"He'll be joining us for dinner. I hope he won't get into the whiskey, too. He likes a tot, but he's on call tonight. Meredith will have the usual Christmas brawls, fuelled by excess liquid cheer, resulting in bloody noses and bruises. But Steven's a sensible chap."

"Do you think anything will come of this thing with Allison?"

"I believe so. They might get engaged over Christmas. Or so Allison says."

"Gladdie will go ballistic."

"How unfortunate."

"You're all for it, then?"

"He's perfect for Allison. And dare I say it? She suits him too. I thought at first she should wait, having just been divorced. But what is the point? She does want to graduate first, which is a good thing. She'll have some independence then, which she didn't have with Joe."

"I feel almost sorry for Joe," I said.

"That's the Christmas cheer talking," Marion said.

I liked Steven right away. Marion was right: he and Allison seemed made for each other. They even looked alike with their reddish hair and freckles. He was in his late thirties, but at first glance he looked like a boy. He had kind, grey eyes, and when he shook my hand I immediately had the feeling that he was someone I could trust my life to. It wasn't a bad feeling for a physician to evoke.

"My favourite sister-in-law," Allison quipped. I was, of course, her only sister-in-law. But the old Allison had always had an edge when she said similar things, a sarcastic bite. The new Allison was softer. She and Steven smiled at each other, and the quick intimate look that passed between them was comradely, best friends as well as lovers.

And I loved Steven's accent. I'm a sucker for the Scottish burr. My friend, Millicent, who claimed to have been married to Edward VIII, had been of Scottish descent, and another friend,

Scottie McGrath, who looked after Conrad if we had to go away, spoke with the Scottish burr.

"Well, lass, it is good to meet you." Steven's hand was small, but his shake was firm.

Peter was asleep on the couch. Hugh was snoring in the armchair. Marion didn't look pleased, but the tree lights were on and how could she say anything in that Christmas setting?

Gracie was in the kitchen, putting the finishing touches on the meal. Gracie was looking after everything, Allison said, sliding her arm through Steven's.

"I hope you met Peter before he passed out," I told Steven. "He doesn't usually drink this much."

"It is Christmas, after all," Steven said, "and yes, I did meet him. I am hoping to come south with Allison to see your bookstore."

"I could use a drink myself," I said, sitting down beside Peter, who rolled over to make room for me.

"I'll get it," Allison said. "Steven and I are sticking to tea since he's on call," she added.

Having been known as the cookbook lady for years, I have achieved a reputation as a pretty decent cook, but Gracie came up with something I had never made: Lobster Newburg. She had actually brought along cans of frozen lobster tails. To remember Maine, she said. There were fresh strawberries for dessert, and she had made Parker House rolls like Gram used to bake. She had also brought the wine, a sparkling rosé.

"You've spoiled us," Marion told Gracie after the strawberries. "I haven't had lobster in years."

"And I did not expect to be eating lobster on Christmas Eve in the wilderness of northern Ontario," Steven commented. "I had no idea what treats would be awaiting me."

Allison giggled.

"But after this," Marion went on to Gracie, "you're to be the guest. You're to enjoy your holiday and relax, not cook for this big crew."

"We'll all be back to stew once the goose is cooked. You'll be eating slops like the rest of us," Hugh cheerfully told Gracie. "Slops it'll be."

"Slops indeed," Marion said.

"Don't listen to Hugh," I said to Gracie. "Marion's a wonderful cook."

"And a dishwasher," Marion said. "I'll do the washing up since you cooked," she told Gracie.

"But we're not through yet. There's the cognac!"

Gracie had brought a bottle of cognac with her.

## Chapter Three

Gladdie was definitely into the Christmas cheer when Marion and I picked the boys up at ten. "Marion— Carolyn! Why do we have to be enemies?"

She began to cry as she embraced us.

"You know I have nothing against you, don't you? Why can't we all be happy the way we used to be? It's not fair. Life is so sad, and it's Christmas, too!"

Carollers were singing on the large television screen in Gladdie's living room. Joe was assembling a plastic fort on the floor with Timmy and Jody. Matthew, holding a new baseball mitt, sat on the couch. Gladdie had covered her arborite coffee table with foil wrap and glued cotton batting on for snow balls, but the foil was torn and a bottle of rum sat beside a plastic Santa in his sleigh.

Matthew smiled wanly at me and Joe ignored his mother, who was insisting that Marion and I remove our coats. "It's Christmas Eve! If you can't let bygones be bygones on Christmas Eve, when can you? Can't you sit down, just for five minutes?"

"Ma," Joe said.

"Joe hasn't even finished the fort yet. The boys want their fort finished. Wasn't it great of Santa to come early?" She swooped down on the boys and gave each of them a big kiss. "And why didn't Allison come?" she asked Marion. "She's been like a daughter to me all these years and she won't even come over on Christmas Eve!"

"I think Allison will be wanting to get the kids to bed," Marion said. "They'll be back on Boxing Day. They can finish the fort then."

"You have to see their presents! Santa brought them all kinds of goodies! Can't you even stay to see their gifts?"

It was eleven before we managed to escape. We wouldn't have a drink? Gladdie directed Joe to plug the kettle in. We could at least have a cup of tea and sample Gladdie's Christmas cake! Were we mad at her, too? We were commanded to tell Allison "Merry Christmas."

"I've got nothing against her, I always said that the divorce was none of my doing," Gladdie went on, crying again, while Joe patiently finished the fort.

Maybe we could all come for dinner on Boxing Day? Even Allison's boyfriend would be welcome!

"Wouldn't he be welcome, Joe?"

Joe didn't answer, which caused a fresh rush of tears. Joe blamed her for the divorce, Gladdie whimpered; Joe never talked to her. Allison had always been better to her than Joe was.

And so on.

Gladdie stood in the doorway and watched, crying, as we piled into Marion's car.

Which would not start. "Damn!" Marion kept turning the key in the ignition but the car only gave a weak wheeze.

"We'll have to phone Peter or Hugh," I said, glancing at the doorway.

But Peter and Hugh would be over the limit, I realized. Hugh had been thumping out carols on the old upright piano, and Peter, the Christmas curmudgeon, having sipped a lot of Gracie's Crown Royal, had been singing "Silent Night" when we left.

Allison wouldn't want to come to Gladdie's. Steven would be a disaster. Gracie didn't know the area, and anyway, she had been drinking, too.

Were any taxis running?

But Joe was coming out.

He would give us a boost, he said.

But it wasn't the battery. Marion's gas tank was empty!

"But I just had it filled and we only went downtown today! Why didn't I notice the gauge was down?"

Joe had been taciturn, but now he grinned. Women and cars!

"I could siphon gas from the truck, but maybe it'd be easier if I just ran you home," he said. "You must have a leak or something."

So Joe drove us home in his truck. Marion's leaking gas tank provided an enthralling topic of conversation.

Hugh and Peter were asleep. Allison's hair was still wet from her shower and she was furious. Steven's beeper had gone while she was in the shower, and Gracie went with him to make his home visit!

"Upstairs and into your pyjamas!" she barked at the boys, who knew better than to argue.

The old Allison was back as she poured herself a drink from what remained in one of the Crown Royal bottles.

"I'll kill that bitch! Waltzing in here and going off with Steven the minute my back is turned! Why'd you have to invite her?" she asked me angrily.

Marion made soothing noises. Peter opened an eye on the couch and turned over.

"Just sneaked out with her, the bastard!" Allison said. "Didn't say one word to me." She took a drink. "Well, Merry Christmas!"

"How do you know Gracie went with Steven?" I asked. "Maybe she went for a walk?"

"Because your precious Gracie told Peter she was going with Steven, that's why! Your lovely Gracie with her painted face!"

"Maybe he didn't know how to say no," I suggested. "He probably didn't know how to get out of it."

"I'll kill both of them!" Allison cried and burst into tears.

"For heaven's sake, Allison, get hold of yourself. It's not as if they've eloped!" Marion told her. "It's Christmas."

"Christmas is ruined!" Allison wailed.

"It will be ruined if you make a scene." Marion scooped up glasses from the top of the piano. "Don't take on so. Pull yourself together before Steven gets back. Don't be a childish, jealous virago now."

"She's trying to get Steven for herself! The way she was looking at him and getting him to talk about himself. Oh, he was lapping it up all right! 'Oh, you're so fascinating, so winderful,'" Allison mimicked. "I am going to kill him! He's asked me to marry him, so what's he doing traipsing around all over town with that slut?"

Marion frowned at ring marks on the piano.

"It'll be all over town that Steven has someone else!"

"Never mind. Go upstairs and see to the boys. We still have stockings to fill. Don't ruin the boys' Christmas, too!"

Allison flounced off, muttering.

"Well, that does take the cake," I said. "I don't blame Allison for being angry. The way Gracie sneaked off is what gets to me! I wish I hadn't invited her."

"She'll be gone soon enough," Marion sighed.

I poked Peter.

"How come Gracie went with Steven?"

"Huh?" He shook his head and looked at me blearily.

"What happened? How come Gracie went with Steven on his call?"

"She just put her coat on and went. Said something about wanting to see Steven at work. I don't know."

"Steven must be a total nerd to take her with him. Couldn't he say no? Why didn't you make some excuse to keep Gracie here? You know how Allison gets."

"Me? What could I do?"

"A lot. Gracie seems to have found all you men so interesting! And what about your father?"

"Went to bed." Peter closed his eyes.
"Get up and help me fill the stockings."

"I am going to say something to Gracie," I told Marion in the kitchen, after we had hung the stockings. I had poured each of us a glass of wine. Peter had gone upstairs to bed and Allison was in the living room, watching the road for Steven's four-by-four. "I am so sorry I invited her, Marion. She's just taken over!"

"I hope Allison doesn't make a scene when they get back," Marion said. "I don't imagine it was Steven's fault. Gracie probably insisted on going with him and there was no polite way he could get out of it. Perhaps it would be better if you didn't say anything to her, Carolyn. Why make something out of this?"

"I'll be glad when she's gone. It was a mistake inviting her. It was just an impulse thing." I thought about telling Gracie about Neil. Gracie seemed to have the ability to make you say things. "She's really rather pathetic, though, trying to get into everyone's good books."

"She's not succeeding very well," Marion said. "Except with the men."

"What I can't understand is why she has to act that way. She ended up with good parents, a real family..."

"But she's not spending Christmas with them, is she?"

"I never thought of that."

"You only know what she's told you," Marion said.

"What do you mean?"

"Maybe she's made a lot of things up," Marion said. "She's so gushy, so flamboyant. What if she is not a teacher? She could be anything."

"But the long story about her Nan. All the details. And she's so self-assured... I think her early life affected her. She told me she's been in therapy."

"So she's crazy," Allison said from the doorway. She slumped down at the kitchen table and poured some wine into her glass.

"Half the world's in therapy these days," I told Allison.

"She's a slut, if you ask me. Sneaking off like that! Steven's never once asked me to go with him on his cases before."

"And I'm sure he didn't ask Gracie," Marion said. "Just don't let on it bothers you."

"I'll do whatever I want," Allison said childishly. "I'm not playing any games. I'm as angry as I've ever been in my life and Steven's going to know it!"

"You should go to bed," Marion said. "We should all go to bed. The boys will be up at the crack of dawn and I promised Hilary someone would collect her by ten. And I'll have to do something about my car.

"You'll see things differently in the morning," she told Allison.

But Allison insisted on staying up until Steven and Gracie returned. "I won't be able to sleep a wink until they're back," she said.

The boys thumped on our door at six-thirty. I jumped out of bed and peeked outside. Steven's vehicle was there at least. I hadn't heard any yelling, so perhaps Allison had taken her mother's advice about not making a scene. Or maybe I had just slept through the noise.

"Merry Christmas," Peter said, motioning for me to return

to bed. Which I did. "Next year let's celebrate Christmas by ourselves at home," he said, kissing me. Conrad's tail bumped on the bed. He recognized the word "home."

"So you remember last night," I said.

"In living colour. I made a fool of myself singing and Gracie kissed me under the mistletoe. Then you went to get the boys with Mom and Gracie took off with Steven."

"Who's back. I saw his car. I wonder if there were any fireworks from Allison. I didn't hear a thing."

"Nor did I. Conrad would have heard and he was quiet, too."

"Get up, you lazy bones!" Matthew called from the hall. "Get up so we can get our loot!"

"Doesn't someone have to pick up that Hilary?" Peter swung his legs out of bed. "I've got half a headache. No booze for me today. Let's take Conrad for a run and pick up Hilary on the way. Get away from the rat pack for a while."

"You're such a curmudgeon," I said. "But all right. Let's do it."


Gracie wasn't there while the boys tore open their gifts and no one mentioned her. Allison was pale and Steven was quiet. Too quiet. I noticed that Allison kept glancing anxiously at him, but she held her tongue.

Steven gave Allison a cassette player and a sweater. She looked disappointed. Had she been expecting an engagement ring? I wondered. She kissed Steven when she thanked him and for a moment the old intimacy was back, but then Steven turned away.

Gracie, wearing a scarlet robe, appeared just as I was unwrapping Marion's gift, a handknit sweater and matching socks. She grimaced as she sat on the couch. She'd made up her face, but she looked tired and apprehensive as Marion handed a package to her. We hadn't opened any of the gifts she'd bought.

Gracie unwrapped Marion's mittens and hat. Tears filled her eyes.

"I want to apologize to everyone," she said, "especially to Steven. I went overboard last night."

Allison bit her lip. So there had been a scene.

"I had no business putting you in that position, Steven, and I can understand how you feel, Allison. I should leave. I've ruined your Christmas. It's no excuse, but I had too much to drink and I got carried away."

Then, of course, Marion had to say, "Nonsense. Of course you mustn't leave. It's Christmas!" She passed Gracie another parcel.

Steven turned red and avoided Allison's eye.


Peter was right. It was wonderful to get away. After we had opened our gifts and emptied our stockings, and after a breakfast of croissants, orange juice and coffee (nothing big this morning, the kitchen was needed for the goose), we put Conrad in the car and drove to the woods, which in Meredith meant a five minute drive.

We would collect Hilary, fill Marion's VW's gas tank on the way back, and one of us would drive her bug home.

We didn't mention Gracie or her extravagant, over-the-top gifts: a leather briefcase, a silk caftan, bath salts, a scarf, and two cookbooks for me; a wine rack, lithograph of an old bookstore, and a fisherman's sweater for Peter. AND an enormous nylon bone and squeaky plastic telephone for Conrad.

Conrad had insisted on bringing the bone with him, and he wouldn't relinquish it so we could throw it, but he raced along the logging path happily. He dropped the bone several times, but snapped it up before we could touch it.

After half an hour of this, we drove to the Meredith Hotel and picked Hilary up. She was a thin, worried looking young woman in her twenties, completely colourless in her navy nylon jacket. She was from Orillia, a couple of hours north of Toronto, and had landed in Meredith a year ago to get away from her abusive husband. She had originally had a summer job with Marion and Hugh's friends, the Swensons, who owned the lodge (and where we were invited for Boxing Day). When the season ended, she had waitressed until Marion hired her.

She looked pinched and distinctly un-Christmas-like, although she brightened when Peter said we had some gifts for her—translate half-a-dozen romance paperbacks.

"It's an awful lot of trouble for you to pick me up," she said, inching away from Conrad, who was trying to lick her face.

"Conrad! Push him away," I told Hilary. "And it's no trouble getting you. No trouble at all."

"You gave us a good excuse to escape the madhouse," Peter said. "We even got to take Conrad for a run!"


The merriness and cosiness of the night before was gone from Gladdie's house. The curtains were drawn and there wasn't even smoke coming from the chimney. Maybe they had let the fire go out, I thought, and were still asleep.

"Someone should tell them we're getting Marion's car," I said, "or they'll think it's stolen."

It took a good five minutes before Gladdie answered the door. She had been asleep, and her grey hair was tousled, her face suspicious. Over her shoulder I could see the debris, the wrapping paper and glasses, of last night.

"You tell Allison to stay away after this," she said.

"What?"

"Coming here in the middle of the night and getting Joe all worked up! So her fancy doctor's left her, has he?" Gladdie smirked. "Driving around, looking for him! Thinking she could get Joe back when the Limey's ditched her!"

"I don't think—"

"You tell her to stay away!"

Gladdie slammed the door.

I wish I could say that dinner was festive, but an unspoken reticence among the adults hung over the table, despite the golden goose, turnip casserole, peas and carrots, jellied salad, mashed potatoes and Brussels sprouts. There were even paper hats and crackers which we pulled after the steamed Christmas pudding and traditional hard sauce.

Gracie didn't say much, and when she talked, it was mostly to Hilary, who, I was annoyed to see, hung onto every word. Hilary was the only one drinking any amount of wine and her pale cheeks were flushed as I heard Gracie inviting her to visit Chicago.

Hilary was giggling by the time the women relaxed in the living room while the men coped with the dishes. But at least this gave me the opportunity to speak to Allison.

"Gladdie says you turned up there last night," I said in a low voice.

"The bitch. She was outside throwing up when I drove by. I shouldn't have stopped."

"So you actually went out looking for Steven?" I whispered.

"It was three in the morning and they still weren't back. I had to do something."

Gracie glanced in our direction.

"What time did they turn up?"

"Four," Allison whispered, but then she noticed Gracie looking at us. Allison shrugged. "It was four when you and Steven got back, wasn't it?" she asked Gracie.

Gracie said: "Mea culpa."

"Shit!" Allison jumped up and went into the kitchen, slamming the door.

She emerged five minutes later with Steven and took their coats out of the hall closet. They were going for a drive, Allison said.

Allison and Steven were gone for two hours and when they returned, Allison was wearing a diamond ring on her left hand.

# Chapter Four

Going to the Swensons on Boxing Day was like starting Christmas all over again.

Bill and Linda Swenson had purchased the big lodge outside Meredith two years before, and a friendship had quickly developed between them and my in-laws. They were more or less in the same business, but not competitors, as one often referred customers to the other. Marion would suggest the Olde Canada Lodge to people who wanted regular meals or more privacy, and Linda kept the bed-and-breakfast in mind for tourists who wanted something less pricey.

Linda and Bill were originally from Minnesota and I liked what they had done to the lodge. It had once been owned by Germans, who had decorated in a heavy, Teutonic style. Linda and Bill had retained the wooden interior, and displayed wood carvings from Quebec, prairie Mennonite quilts and depression glass. The furniture was pine replicas of pioneer originals. Linda was a talented printmaker and her abstract work hung on the walls.

They were in their early sixties, both sturdy in a blonde Scandinavian kind of way, outdoorsy and capable, but up on things. *The New Yorker*, the *Times Literary Supplement* and Canadian magazines such as *This* and *Canadian Forum* were piled in the comfortable main room with its big stone hearth.

Bill and Linda had decided to be closed for Christmas, although they had a full house booked for New Year's. We were the only guests. A fire burned brightly in the grate and beside it, a gigantic evergreen was covered with tiny red lights, Scandinavian straw ornaments and white origami birds.

The cheer was helped by the fact that Gracie, pleading a headache, had stayed at Marion's. The boys were at Joe's, but Steven was here for the brunch, although he had to leave by three to make the rounds in the hospital.

The big news, of course, was Allison and Steven's engagement. Bill brought up a bottle of champagne from the wine cellar.

"May happiness be yours!" Bill toasted. He was a big man, with a blonde beard streaked with grey. Linda sometimes called him Eric the Red, and she had done a funky print of him in a Viking boat.

"Happiness and wealth!"

"And health," Hugh added, "although you'll be able to do your own doctoring."

"Physician heal thyself, is that it?" Steven joked.

Whatever had happened with Gracie appeared to be forgotten. Allison kept inspecting her ring and smiling at Steven, who seemed pretty pleased himself.

They would be married in June, Allison explained as we sat down to crepes filled with grilled chicken, lox on crispy rye bread, orange and wild rice salad and a variety of cold cuts and cheese.

"We haven't made up our minds about whether to buy or build," Allison said. "Steven likes those prefabricated log houses, but we probably couldn't be in it by June. There isn't much available in Meredith right now and Steven's place will be kind of tight for all of us."

"When you're in love you can live in a tent," Linda said. "We spent our honeymoon in a tent in Alaska, actually."

"Really? Is that a fact?" Steven looked interested.

"Don't get any ideas," Allison told him. "We're going to Scotland for our honeymoon. We'll go when school's out so the kids can stay with you," she said to Marion. "Scotland and maybe a side trip to France, right, Steven?"

"The Highlands and the high life," Steven said.

It was really a wonderful meal, and afterwards, we opened presents by the tree. It had started to snow heavily outside and the swirling snowflakes against the large window were a contrast to the red tree lights.

Linda and Bill's presents were mostly homemade: small prints Linda had made which Bill had framed, jars of currant jelly and mustard relish, walking sticks Bill had whittled. There were books for Allison's boys, and there was even a package to be taken home for Gracie.

Hot rum punch appeared. Steven had a glass before leaving for the hospital.

The nice thing about being at Linda and Bill's was that you could relax. While the wedding talk continued, I leafed through the periodicals— Peter carried most of them in The Bookworm, but I had gotten behind in reading them— and no one minded. Linda had prepared a list of books for Peter to order for her and Bill; a decent bookstore was the one thing she missed up north, she often said.

The heat from the fire and the hot rum soon put me to sleep. When I awoke, Allison was telling everyone about Steven's predicament with Gracie. Now that the fight had been made up and she was safely and happily engaged, she made light of the whole thing.

"I mean, there's the poor man trying to put his coat and boots on so he can visit this eighty-five-year-old woman in the boondocks whose ancient husband has called to say he's afraid that Mother won't make it through the night! It was only gas pains, but how was Steven to know that? And there's this pushy female reeking of perfume and whiskey who announces it has always been her lifetime ambition to see a country doctor at his work! She just plain waltzed out of the door with him and sat herself down in his car!

"Oh, I was angry at the time, but he made her wait in the car and I can just imagine Gracie freezing her buns off in the middle of nowhere! And then, on the way home, his beeper goes off again and it's over to Meredith General where Gracie trails in his wake. She actually sat in the waiting room with the husband of the woman giving birth! Chatted up the nurses and what have you! Steven was so embarrassed! 'Ever so embarrassed,' is what he said. You know the sexy way he talks. I don't know what Carolyn was thinking of when she invited that dame."

I closed my eyes again.

"Carolyn had no idea what she'd be like," Peter said loyally.

"You didn't think she was so bad yourself Christmas Eve," Allison went on. "Letting her sit on your lap."

"I didn't let her!" Peter protested. "She just kind of dropped there!"

"Yeah, and you pushed her away, didn't you?"

"I suppose you were up to no good, too," Marion told Hugh. "Did she sit on your lap?"

"She certainly did not!"

"What were the two of you doing together in the kitchen for so long?"

"We were making a salad," Hugh said rather pompously. And loudly. Marion pointed out that I was asleep.

"I heard every word," I said, and looked at Peter, who blushed.

"It's a wonder she didn't squish you," I said. "She must weigh fifty pounds more than you!"

"And sixty pounds at least more than Steven!" Allison hooted.

"I've never heard it called making a salad before," Marion mused.

"Bring your Gracie 'round," Bill suggested. "Maybe we'll hire her."

"The Olde Canada Brothel," Linda suggested. "Or something with more tone? The Olde Canada Gentleman's Establishment? We could take out ads in *The New Yorker*."

"Sitting on your lap," I told Peter. "Shame on you! Couldn't you have pushed her off or something?"

I was only kidding, but Peter's face darkened. "Wait till you hear what she said about you," he blurted out.

"What? What?" Allison's ears were keen.

There was a moment of embarrassed silence until everyone, once again, began suggesting ludicrous names for Bill and Linda's brothel in the woods.

They were still joking like this when we left at five. We had taken two cars, and finally I was able to ask Peter what Gracie had said about me, but he would not tell me.

"It was nothing, forget it. I don't want to discuss it."

"I think I know what it was." Neil Andersen, I thought; Gracie, damn her, must have repeated my flippant, wine-talking remark about Neil!

Except, maybe, it wasn't so flippant.

Peter looked at me sharply.

"I still don't want to talk about it," Peter said.

"I told her all kinds of stupid things the first night she was in Meredith when we stayed up and talked. Just silly stuff. What they used to call 'girl talk.'"

"I don't believe it anyway," Peter said.

"What? What didn't you believe?"

"She hinted that you had an affair."

"I'm going to kill her," I said.

But I didn't have to kill Gracie. She was still breathing when we got home, but someone had nearly done her in.

# Chapter Five

She lay there, beside the Christmas tree, on Marion's new green couch. Her legs were sprawled apart, half on the couch and half off, and her eyes were closed. There was a gash on her forehead and an abrasion on her cheek. Her head was tilted at an odd angle, twisted up on the armrest of the sofa, as though she'd fallen against it. There was blood on the upholstery. That was all I could think of: Marion would have to have the sofa dry-cleaned.

But Hugh's police training asserted itself. He felt Gracie's pulse and ordered Marion to call 911. Within seconds, his mouth clamped over Gracie's as he pushed air into her lungs. There was a gurgle, and then he straightened Gracie out and tilted her head back. He knelt beside her and pinched her nose as he breathed in and allowed the air to escape.

Gracie's eyes remained closed. In, out, in, out. I noticed the Christmas lights were on, although we'd shut them off before leaving.

Behind me, Peter's knees buckled. I had to help him up.

"Breathe, Gracie, keep breathing," Marion repeated over and over.

The ambulance seemed to take forever. A vehicle stopped outside, but it was Joe returning the boys. "Jesus." Joe took one look, ordered the boys to go upstairs, and bent to relieve Hugh.

Allison loosened the belt of Gracie's dress and cradled her head.

Peter sat on a dining-room chair with his head between his knees.

Hugh went outside to await the ambulance, which arrived in

a great flurry of lights and sirens. I recognized one of the volunteer firemen, someone Peter had gone to school with, who immediately ripped Gracie's dress and placed a rubber plunger type of thing on Gracie's chest.

"Everyone out. Get everyone out of here," he ordered, but he allowed Allison to remain and hold Gracie's head.

The ambulance was followed by Hugh's replacement, Chief of Police Guy Boudreau, who decided immediately to call in the Ontario Provincial Police. We were told to sit in the kitchen and not to touch anything.

"Jesus." Joe mopped his brow. "What a thing to happen over Christmas. I take it she's your friend who came up from the States."

"Gracie."

"The boys talked about her. What on earth happened? Heart attack, you figure, or what?"

Marion shrugged. She was very pale, and her hand shook as she fiddled with the buttons on her coat. "All I know is we found her like that. We were out at the lodge today for brunch. She said she had a headache and stayed home."

"Headache. Maybe she had a stroke," Joe mused.

There was activity in the hall. They were taking Gracie away in the ambulance.

Hugh came into the kitchen.

"I'll follow in the car." He hadn't obeyed orders to leave the living room. "Guy's going to want to talk to all of us, take statements."

"But what happened?" I asked.

"Too early to tell. That head looks suspicious."

"I'm coming to the hospital, too," I said. "She's my friend. She's going to make it, isn't she?"

Hugh didn't answer at once. "She's still breathing, that's the main thing," he said at last. "If you can find her purse, you might want to bring that along. They'll need some ID at the hospital."

Allison had gone with Gracie in the ambulance, and we sat together in the waiting room. It was just a tiny place, two rows of red vinyl chairs and a scratched wooden table that held old *Reader's Digest* and *Time*.

"I wish Steven had been there," she said, twisting her new ring.

"He'll be along soon." The nurse on duty had reported that Steven had received a call at the hospital to see a patient, but that he'd likely check in as soon as possible. In the meantime, she'd keep trying to get him on his pager.

"He's going to stop making so many house-calls once we're married," Allison said. "I'll be fielding the calls, too. Half of them are for nothing. People take advantage of softies like Steven."

"Do you think Gracie will make it?" I didn't want to discuss Steven now.

Allison nodded. "She doesn't look like someone ready to die. There's a look. Open mouth, staring eyes. The first time I saw it, I went around imagining how everyone would look like that."

"I know she's not Miss Popularity, but who would bash her head in?"

"I would have, the other night," Allison admitted, "but I have a pretty tight alibi, wouldn't you say? Anyway, I wouldn't actually do it. I couldn't kill anyone. Besides, she could have had a heart attack or seizure and hit her head on the table when she fell. It's too early to say." She frowned. "You should have looked in her purse."

But Hugh had taken it.

"Something's not right with her, even if she did have a heart attack," Allison said. "Doesn't it strike you odd that she gave everyone fabulous gifts, but the boys got paint-by-number sets and easy puzzles they're much too old for?"

"Maybe she figured she'd bought enough. Maybe she doesn't care for kids."

"But she's a teacher. Okay, I can see some teachers getting fed up with kids, but they should have some idea of what kids of certain ages like. It doesn't add up." She looked at her watch and wondered if she should try calling Steven herself at home. He might have left his pager in the car, or the batteries might be dead. Or something.

"He'll be here soon."

"She did try to get him into the sack," Allison said, turning to me. "They went to his place because she had to go to the bathroom. Or so she said. They had a drink there. But Steven said nothing happened, and I believe him."

"I shouldn't have invited her."

Allison shrugged.

"She's not the way I imagined she'd be." Or was she? I wondered. Gracie had always been forceful... In a weird way, that confident voice on the phone had prompted me to invite her. There was something about her. It was difficult to explain. She was the kind of person it was hard to say no to, I thought, as old Doctor Walker appeared in the waiting room. He nodded at us and settled his skinny frame into a chair.

"We've got her stabilized," he said, "but we have to run some tests."

"She'll be all right, then? She'll make it?" I asked.

"Too early to say. She hasn't regained consciousness. Would you happen to know anything about any drug addictions?"

"What???"

"We noticed track marks."

"Are you kidding?" Beside me, Allison let out something very much like a snort. I ignored her. "She drank a lot over Christmas, in a festive kind of way, but I never noticed anything like drugs. You mean injections? Heroin, crack?" There'd been a lot of crack cocaine around Guelph lately, but Gracie in no way resembled the wraiths of young girls who stood on street corners. "I can't believe it of her," I said. "Maybe she's a diabetic."

"You don't have track marks from diabetes," Allison explained. "You inject yourself in the thigh or belly, just under the skin."

"What other surprises do you have for us?" she asked Walker.

"We'll know more after the tests are done. You wouldn't happen to know her next-of-kin, would you?" he asked me.

"I'm afraid I don't. She spoke about her adopted parents. Their name must be Forbes, the same as hers. That was what it said on her ID, wasn't it? Gracie Forbes?"

"That's what her driver's license said. But there wasn't anything about next-of-kin, or anyone to contact."

"I don't even know where her parents live. She said she taught at a private school around Chicago, but that's not much help, is it? Even if I knew the name of the school, there'd be no one there over the holidays."

Hugh came in and sat down heavily. His face looked drained.

"Dr. Walker says Gracie has track marks on her arm," I blurted to him. "This is all my fault, for inviting her!"

"You had nothing to do with it," Allison said, but this was said sharply, impatiently.

I stood up and said I wanted to see Gracie. Just for a minute,

Walker agreed. As I left the waiting room, I heard Dr. Walker telling Hugh that Gracie's injuries were definitely the result of a severe blow to the head.

"The police should be prepared to lay murder charges," Dr. Walker said. "We doubt she's going to make it."

They had Gracie in a private room. Her face was still, immobile, heavy, and there were tubes everywhere. She was hooked up to a heart monitor and she was getting oxygen. A thick bandage covered the right side of her temple. Her heavy breathing filled the room. You could still see make-up on her face, but this quiet, still face reminded me of the young Gracie. Suddenly I had an image of Gracie and me at the beach; of Gracie and me sitting on the verandah in Maine.

"Gracie? It's going to be all right. I'm going to try and contact your parents."

Gracie gurgled. The nurse adjusted the aspirating tube.

"She seemed to react," I said to the nurse.

"It's just a reflex, but you never know. People come out of comas and it's surprising what they remember."

I took that as encouragement, and I sat down beside Gracie's bed and talked to her about Maine, but the gurgling was not repeated. In— out— in— out: I listened to her breathing and watched the needle on the heart machine.

The hospital gown covered her arms past the elbows. I didn't want to see the needle marks.

"Gracie, I don't know what happened or why or what you've done, but it doesn't matter. Just listen to me. Remember when you wanted to be a nun? You wore this white towel, probably stolen from the Holiday Inn, and you were grinning from ear to ear the first time I saw you. Remember? I was this skinny little girl and you seemed so wise to me, so sophisticated..."

Hugh appeared in the room.

"I think I'll remain with her," I said.

"We're all staying out at the lodge," he said. "They've brought in the investigation unit. Taking photos and dusting for fingerprints. They'll likely be wanting to talk to you."

"We have to try to find her parents."

"The police will do that." He looked at Gracie. "I suppose it wouldn't hurt for you to stay."

"What do you mean, an investigation unit?" But I knew. I thought of what I had overheard Dr. Walker say.

"They have their suspicions. That gash didn't come by itself." He nodded at the bandage. "You're all right to stay, then? I'll send Peter, shall I?"

"It doesn't matter. Where's Allison?"

"Gone to Steven's place. To rouse him, she says. She thinks he's fallen asleep. Can I get you anything?"

"Tell Peter to bring me something to read."

It was going to be a long night.

It was a long night. I asked to see Gracie's purse, but it had already been turned over to the police. I sat beside Gracie's bed until the rhythmic sounds of her breathing almost put me to sleep, and then I went to find some food. The cafeteria was closed, but the nurse hustled up a dish of chili from the hospital kitchen, and I ate that, while the nurse drank tea. Dr. Walker had been called from a family celebration, she said. Son and grandchildren home from Toronto.

Had I met Steven? she wanted to know. Was it true he and Allison were engaged? Everyone liked Steven, although his English ways could be off-putting. He could sound so aristocratic...

"That's just the accent," I said. "And he's Scottish, not English. But I'm a sucker for Scottish accents."

"Going to be a lot of broken hearts when he marries," the nurse said. She was young, in her twenties, but her features were pointy, sharp. Would her heart be broken, too, even if— I noticed her rings— she was married?

"I've seen the ring with my own eyes," I said.

"A diamond? Not a big one, I bet. They say the Scots are stingy."

Gossip helped to take my mind away from Gracie attached to her machines, and we were speculating about how attractive a man could be just because he was a doctor, when Peter arrived with the *Globe and Mail*, the Carol Shields book I had been re-reading, and the Ontario travel book Marion and Hugh had given me for Christmas.

I sat by Gracie's bed and worked on the *Globe* cryptic puzzle while Peter wandered in and out. Gracie's breathing seemed quieter. I wondered about the test results, but Dr. Walker had gone home.

Darkness comes early in the northern winter, and soon the room was dim. And almost cosy. A small artificial tree sat on the window sill and beyond it, in the town, Christmas lights twinkled. I did not mind at all that Peter, as a nurse informed me, had fallen asleep in the waiting room. A nurse came to check from time to time, but Gracie and I were alone.

Until the police came. They took me to an empty office to interview me, but a female officer remained outside of Gracie's room.

What did I actually know about Gracie? I realized, how little that was as Constable Barnovich asked me questions. Other than memories of Maine, every single thing I knew about her, or believed about her, was what Gracie had told me. Barnovich admitted the police had been unsuccessful in reaching Gracie's family, but he would not tell me any more. He tried to hide it, but he did seem incredulous that I did not even know where Gracie taught. (If she taught, I told myself, remembering Allison's words).

Was I aware that Gracie had used morphine?

So the test results were in.

I shook my head.

"I'm just realizing how silly I was to invite her for Christmas," I admitted. "I had no idea she was a drug addict."

How had she gotten along with everyone? Barnovich wanted to know.

I told him the truth.

"Couldn't she have cracked her head when she fell? If she overdosed?"

Barnovich shook his head.

"How did she get along with Dr. MacLeod?"

"Steven? She went on call with him Christmas Eve, very much at her own insistence, from what Allison said. But I only observed her being friendly with him when I was there. I've explained how she pushed herself forward, trying to be everything to everyone. She was like that in Maine, too, as a kid. You'll have to ask Steven."

"Dr. MacLeod seems to have disappeared," Barnovich said.

"Let's go home," Peter said at two in the morning. "Or at least to bed, since bed's at the lodge tonight."

I wanted to stay at the hospital, but I also suddenly wanted a bed. Gracie was stabilized and the hospital would call me immediately if there was any change.

# Chapter Six

Winter sunlight streaming through the hand-woven yellow curtains woke me at nine-thirty. Nine-thirty! I should have dashed for the phone to enquire about Gracie, but the warmth of the lodge bedroom with its pine furniture and red duvet was delicious. I should have been anxious about Gracie, but what I felt, upon awakening, was exhaustion and dread. Gracie, Gracie go away. Trouble and more trouble. In that comfortable room, Gracie's misfortune seemed, illogically, to be her own fault.

I didn't even have a change of clothes with me, I realized as I swung my feet out of bed. The green dress I'd worn yesterday lay on the foot of the bed.

I could hear Conrad barking outside. It was his "throw-the-stick" bark, and I knew even before I parted the curtains that Peter had him outside to play fetch.

Bill was getting out of his Landrover with Hilary, I saw. Conrad was so taken with the stick that Peter held in the air that he didn't even bound over.

How was Gracie?

Had Steven turned up?

I decided to have a shower before finding out.

"Oh, dear," Marion said when she saw me. "I threw a few things into a bag, but with all the fuss and to-do, I'm afraid I didn't think to find a fresh outfit for you. Maybe you can nip over on your way to the hospital."

Linda poured me a cup of coffee. A table had been laid in part of the main dining room. An egg cup, covered with a quilted cosy, was beside my plate and a basket held muffins and rolls.

"I could lend you a pair of jeans, but I doubt if they'd fit," Linda said, patting her thighs, as she sat down beside Marion.

"I'm hoping we'll be able to return home this afternoon," Marion said. "So much trouble for you, Linda. A couple from New York are arriving this afternoon," she informed me.

"Always room in the inn," Linda said. "Ah, Hilary. I'm so glad you were able to come to help out. Sit down and have a coffee with us."

Hilary looked tired and pale and her grey sweater did nothing to cheer her up as she accepted a cup of coffee.

We sat quietly for a minute.

"I'm almost afraid to ask," I said.

"Hugh phoned the hospital at eight. Gracie is the same," Marion said. "She hasn't regained consciousness."

"No word on her family, I suppose."

Marion shook her head.

"And Steven?"

"Hugh and Allison are searching the back roads. He had a call to make in Hibernia, apparently, and the snow ploughs didn't go out there last night. He could he stuck in a ditch. At least he'll have a blanket and a candle. I made sure he had the basic northern driving kit when the first snow came. Allison is out of her mind with worry, as you can imagine."

"Where are the boys?"

"At Joe's. He took them for the night. It seemed the best thing all around."

"I suppose I'll go to the hospital after breakfast. Maybe I should check the library, too. Look at telephone directories."

"I'm sure the police have tried that," Linda said. "And is the library even open today?"

"It was closed for Boxing Day, but it's open today," Hilary said and blushed. She bit into a muffin. "I have my name down for the new Danielle Steele."

"I suppose your Christmas books are finished," Marion teased.

Hilary blushed again. Linda gave me the smallest wink. Hilary and her trashy romance novels.

Linda lit a rare cigarette and blew the smoke away. The gesture made me think of Allison. I had a terrible feeling.

Gracie was still in intensive care and the same female police officer sat by the door. She was reading *Maclean's*, which she didn't try to hide.

"The doctor's with her now. If you could wait a minute—"

"Dr. MacLeod?" My voice rose with hope.

The officer shook her head.

"Allison and her father are looking for him," I explained. "He had a call out at Hibernia last night and the snow ploughs didn't go through."

"Nor did we, I'm afraid. We patrol most of the back roads, but Hibernia was blocked, as you say."

"Someone could freeze out there."

"It's not likely. There are houses all along the road. It has happened, of course, but Dr. MacLeod knows the area and would have made it to a house." She smiled at me. "But I suppose he could have gotten stuck. Or lost. It even happens in southern Ontario. Not only in the wild north."

Her name was Sarah and she was originally from Toronto, I learned. We were still chatting when the door to Gracie's room opened and Dr. Walker came out, followed by a barrel-chested, bearded man he introduced as Dr. Bradley, a neurologist from North Bay.

"How's Gracie doing?"

Dr. Walker let Dr. Bradley do the talking.

"Miss Forbes is still unconscious. She's sustained a skull fracture on the right temple, which is complicated by morphine ingestion. We're going to have a kidney man look at her. She appears to be in the early stages of diabetes, which complicates matters."

"What do you mean?"

"There's a danger of kidney failure."

"Kidney failure? Diabetes? I can't take this all in!"

"I doubt if she knew about the diabetes. We found a fair amount of alcohol in her system, which is a further complication."

"But for now she's holding her own?"

"For now. We may decide to airlift Miss Forbes to London or Hamilton."

"The next twelve hours will tell," Dr. Walker added.

"Can I see her?"

"Why not?" Bradley shrugged. "Although she won't know you're there."

"Someone should be with her. She doesn't have anyone else here." Sarah had put her magazine away. More exactly, she was sitting on it. "And there's no word on her family," I speculated.

I waited until the doctors had departed before asking Sarah if Gracie's injury was being considered an attempted homicide.

"I'm not just here to read magazines," she said.

"Suspects?"

But Sarah wouldn't, or couldn't, say.

Gracie was the same, although the make-up had been washed off her face. Without it, she looked whiter than white, and again, she reminded me so much of the Gracie I had known in Maine. Her regular breathing filled the room, and the heart monitor was still on, but the breathing tube had been removed.

"Gracie? It's me, Carolyn. I'm here, Gracie."

I sat down beside the bed and noticed Sarah peering into the room. We nodded at each other. My purse was heavy with last night's books, and it was tempting to take out reading material, but it seemed callous to do so.

What if they did airlift Gracie south? I would go with her, I told myself, watching the line on the heart monitor. My grandmother had been hooked up like that before she died. I had been called to Maine. I was living in Guelph with my first husband, Charlie, then. Being a draft dodger, Charlie hadn't been able to come with me, and I'd been alone in the hospital room, just as I was now, waiting for her to die. She had never regained consciousness. She'd suffered irreversible brain damage and the machines had been disconnected, but she kept breathing for a long week.

"Remember my grandmother?" I found myself saying to Gracie. "She died after I was in Canada for a year. I went south to be with her. I wish you had been there, too. I had to arrange the funeral by myself, but Charlie's parents came all the way from New Jersey. His mother didn't like me much, she wasn't like Marion, but I was glad she came. Even if she blamed me for luring her son to Canada."

No response. I touched Gracie's hand. It was cold.

"Charlie's mother was a real old battle-axe," I went on, "and wouldn't leave until she found out about the will! But Gram made her will so that any spouse of mine wouldn't inherit and when Charlie and I divorced, Gram's house remained mine. I still own it, although I have it rented out. When you get better maybe we can take a trip to Maine together. I have this understanding with the tenants that I can stay there. We'll bunk together. Remember how Gram wanted each of us to have a room and you'd sneak into my room and we'd talk all night? You told me all about Reg's girlfriends..."

Peter walked into the room. I shook my head. "I don't know why I'm talking to her, although they say people in comas can hear."

Peter peered at Gracie. I noticed Sarah watching. And so did he. "How about a coffee in the cafeteria? And then I think you should go to Mom's and change your clothes."

"Is it okay?"

"Okay. I checked. Let's have that coffee. I've got news. Not very pleasant news."

"What?"

But he wouldn't tell me until we were seated with mugs of coffee in the cafeteria.

Steven had been seen visiting Marion's house while we were at the lodge. Allison and Hugh hadn't found him. He hadn't turned up to see his patient in Hibernia. He was wanted "for questioning."

"That's awful."

"Yeah." Peter stirred his coffee.

"Poor Allison."

"You can say that again."

"How's she taking it?"

"As badly as only Allison can. She wants to call Steven's folks in Scotland, but Mom won't let her. Dad had to wrestle the phone away from her."

"He certainly didn't strike me as someone who'd hurt anyone. Not the way Gracie was hurt."

"I have a hunch they suspect him of injecting Gracie with morphine," Peter said. "Say she was an addict and he knew it. So he injects her. Tries to do her in."

"But as a doctor he'd know how much to give her. Did you know she's almost a diabetic?" I filled Peter in on what Dr. Bradley had told me. "He wouldn't just give her enough to dope her and then smash her skull in."

"Unless she needed a fix and then they had an argument and he lost it. She could have been blackmailing him or something. She does have a way of getting secrets out of people. Apparently Dad told her all about this tourist last summer, how he was tempted to run away. This German woman. Elise. They sat up drinking wine and quoting poetry. Shakespeare and Heine. Dad said Elise said she fell in love with him."

"That's silly. Booze talk."

"Right. But Dad told Gracie. Mom doesn't know, but Dad told me."

"Somehow I don't think your mother would be surprised."

"Of course she would!"

"Never mind. It doesn't matter."

"It was just stupid talk, but Dad's worried in case Gracie told anyone. And Allison told her about almost going to bed with Joe just before the divorce. She's worried that that's why Steven left. Apparently our Scottish doctor lad's a real Calvinist when it comes to sins of the flesh."

"A nurse last night said Steven is stuck up."

"Maybe Gracie taunted him and he bashed her head in," Peter speculated.

"After he injected her with morphine."

We sat considering this. It seemed completely far-fetched. I just could not imagine Steven hitting someone on the head. Or giving an addict drugs, for that matter.

Unless Gracie, needing a fix, was blackmailing him, as Peter had said.

Steven would want to protect his reputation. His new life. But against what?

"You are right about Gracie getting secrets out of people. What she told you about me was so silly. And she knew it. And to think she had to go and tell, like a tattle-tale child. What did you tell her?"

Peter turned red. It didn't matter, he said. It was nothing.

"Tell. I told her that Neil Andersen was a mighty attractive guy. Now I've told you and you have to tell me."

"I told her about Lorna."

"The girl you lived with in Toronto."

"Right. She looked me up in Guelph and we went for lunch."

"Lorna came to The Bookworm? When was this?"

"About two years ago."

"And you didn't tell me?"

"I thought you'd be upset. Why upset you if it meant nothing?"

"That's exactly why! It meant nothing and you kept it from me!"

"See, you're upset right now."

"Because you kept it a secret! It's the fact that you purposely kept a secret from me that is upsetting! What did she want, anyway?"

"She wanted to go to bed with me and she wanted to buy pot."

"From you? I don't believe it! Peter the dope smoker!"

"Once upon a time, many long years ago. Lorna had just broken up with her boyfriend of the moment and she didn't know anyone else to ask for pot. Know how she found me?"

"How?"

"She read an article about you in a magazine. I was mentioned, along with the store."

"Well the goddamn nerve of her! Didn't she try to throw herself out of the window when you lived in that place off Queen Street because you wouldn't tell her you loved her?"

"Something like that. Ancient history. Do you want to pick up some clean clothes or do you want to hold Gracie's hand?"

I wanted clean clothes.


Marion's house looked dreary. The bright winter sunlight illuminated the dangling electric lights and the ornaments. The tree was beginning to droop and the couch and coffee table had been shifted. The police hadn't cleaned up the powder they had used to test for fingerprints.

Upstairs, the bathroom was a mess, with towels thrown helter-skelter and tubes of make-up cluttering the counter. The same fingerprint dust. I changed my mind about using the shower and quickly threw jeans, tops, clean underwear, and, in case we stayed at the lodge tonight, my Christmas nightgown into a bag.

A cruiser sat on the street. The police were still watching the house.

"Why?" I asked Peter.

But the police hadn't told him anything. Maybe someone suspected there were drugs in the house, Peter speculated.

"Let's stop off at the library," I said. "Hilary told me it's open today."

"What for? You don't have Mom's card, do you?" I often used Marion's card if I wanted to borrow books from the Meredith Public Library. "Wouldn't you rather go to the lodge and get changed?"

"I just want to check the Chicago phone directory."

"I'm sure the police have done that. The library probably doesn't even have American phone directories," Peter said and sighed.

"But the long distance operator won't give listings of businesses. You have to have a name."

"Gracie's school won't have a flowery name," Peter said.

"What do you mean? What're you talking about?"

"I just remembered something. She was talking about all your success. How you were on television and going to schools. 'I'm surprised Carolyn still bothers going to schools now that she's famous,' Gracie said. 'Like having tea at the Lily Becker School.'"

"I never told Gracie about Lily Becker School!" The senior girls at the school had held a tea in my honour because I'd contributed a piece to their magazine. They'd written to thank me for their encouragement and the letter was in my purse! "She must have gone through my handbag and read the letter from the school!"

I rummaged through kleenex, receipts from Christmas and a card I hadn't mailed and found the pale blue envelope that had come from the school.

"Gracie said Lily Becker sounded like a finishing school," Peter said.

"She's not far wrong about that." I threw the letter on the dashboard. "What a sly woman!"

"I thought you'd mentioned it to her. She said her school's name was more distinguished."

"But she didn't tell you the name."

"Cor-rect."

Peter turned the car around towards the library.

Surprisingly, the library was fairly crowded; crowded for Meredith, anyway. When I first came to Meredith, the library had been housed in a room at the town hall, packed with old Victoria Holts and musty paperbacks. The "new" library was really twelve years old, but it had retained its sparkling cleanliness and space. With its larger collection, it was a godsend for Marion, who had lobbied to have a proper library.

There was a line-up at the circulation desk but Carmel

Rossiter, the librarian, gave a wave and a grin. She wrote the odd short story herself, and I'd helped her place one in an anthology about the north which my publisher, Jake Hendricks, had put out.

I checked the telephone directories. New York was there, and Los Angeles, but no Chicago. It was stupid, but while Peter looked at the new titles, I pulled out the New York directory. Lots of Forbes, but I had called the Chicago area code when speaking to Gracie.

"So how are you?" Carmel asked when she was free. "I heard about your friend. Awful." She pulled a face. Carmel was from Toronto and we often joked about how news travelled in Meredith.

"It's terrible, all right. You've heard we're all staying out at the lodge?"

"I should be so lucky. We've got the in-laws and out-laws at our place. I'm hoping they'll be gone soon so Ben and I can go to the lodge for New Year's Eve. They say someone tried to do your friend in. Rumour has it our sexy new doctor did it and took off."

"I can't imagine Steven doing it. I only met him when we came for Christmas, but I liked him. The whole thing's been a disaster. I spent most of the night at the hospital. Haven't even changed from yesterday." I opened my coat to show her my green dress. "And on top of everything, we can't find Gracie's family. I was hoping you'd have a Chicago directory here. I was going to get a list of private schools in the Chicago area."

"No Chicago directory here, I'm afraid, but I can get the information from North Bay for you."

I moved aside to let a woman in a purple coat pass to the desk.

"Could you?" I asked, after the woman was finished. "And could you keep it kind of quiet? I know the police have probably gone that route, but I want to try myself. I know you can't get listings of businesses from the operator. I just want to see the private schools in the Chicago yellow pages."

Carmel nodded as Peter joined us. "They can fax it," Carmel said. "I'll give you a call. You'll still be at the lodge tonight?"

"As far as I know. But wait until morning if you're busy. I wouldn't want to make a lot of long distance calls from the lodge. I didn't even think you'd be open today, but Hilary said you were. You must know Hilary. She reads piles of romances."

"Half the female population reads nothing but romances here," Carmel said. A teenager came up with an armload of Babysitter Club books. "I'll call you later about the fax."

Allison was on the phone to Scotland when we got back to the lodge.

Her prospective mother-in-law told her that Steven had an ex-wife in Toronto.

# Chapter Seven

I thought of calling Neil Andersen. I knew he had some time off between Christmas and New Year's. He planned to be with his daughter in Toronto on Christmas Day, but he was going to spend the rest of his holiday in Guelph "vegging out" from the

Ontario Provincial Police. I hadn't heard from the library. Neil would have been only too glad to sprint into the Guelph Library to look up Chicago area schools in the telephone directory. He might even have been able to use police contacts to dig out information in Chicago.

But speaking to Gracie about him had changed things. I was attracted to Neil. I wasn't planning a red-hot affair, but voicing my attraction to Gracie had made it seem more real. What had been a fancy, a corner of a daydream, now seemed the tiniest bit possible. I had never seriously considered being unfaithful to Peter. I did not want to be unfaithful. I wasn't going to be unfaithful. But, yes, I was drawn to Neil. I felt guilty, even if Peter had confessed a secret of his own.

"Why on earth did you have to tell Peter?" I asked Gracie.

There was no response, just her stillness and her breathing and the whirr of the machines.

"It was stupid talk, late night drinking talk."

Yes, lie there, Miss Innocent, I thought uncharitably, but at least the hospital room was peaceful after the emotional scene at the lodge, with Allison crying and yelling. She had discovered the name of the ex-wife, Sandra MacLeod, and wanted to phone her immediately.

Marion had talked to Steven's mother and learned that Steven had been married eighteen years before, when he was twenty. The marriage was ancient history.

Allison kept dialling Sandra's number and hanging up.

"You have caused a lot of trouble," I whispered to Gracie, as Dr. Walker's face appeared around the door. He nodded at me and bent over her bed.

"How's she doing?"

He shook his head. No change, he said, and they would probably airlift her tomorrow to McMaster Hospital in Hamilton.

"If only we could find her family," I said. "Do you think she'll suffer brain damage?"

"Hard to say in these cases. We revived a woman last year and I thought she'd be a vegetable, but in three days she was sitting up and talking. We never give up hope, but we're concerned about her kidneys."

"Because of the diabetes? I'm sure she didn't know or she wouldn't have had so much to drink over Christmas."

"You'd be surprised what some people will do to their bodies. But you're right. She probably did not know."

"I'll go to Hamilton if she's airlifted, of course."

He nodded.

"And we haven't heard from Steven," I said conversationally; the doctor seemed friendlier today. "I can't imagine Steven being involved."

Dr. Walker gave me a strange look.

"Carolyn?"

Matthew's head appeared at the door.

"Matthew! What on earth?" I asked him in the hall, out of earshot of the police officer— a man, today. "You're supposed to be at your dad's. What're you doing here?"

"I said I was checking Dad's rabbit snares."

"You walked? All the way?"

"It's only three miles. Not even that. They won't miss me. Dad's sleeping and Nan's watching her soaps. I've got to talk to you."

"Let's go to the cafeteria. I could use a coffee anyway."

"Now then," I said, after I had my coffee in front of me and Matthew was staring at his glass of Sprite. "Tell me what's going on."

"You have to promise not to tell, Carolyn."

"You know I never lie to you. But what's this about? Is it to do with Gracie?"

He nodded.

"I don't know if I can promise, Matthew. If you know anything about what happened to Gracie, you have to tell the police. Someone tried to kill her."

He whispered something I couldn't hear.

"Say that again."

This time I just made it out.

"I don't want my father to go to jail."

"Your father?"

"You have to promise."

"Matthew, what do you know?"

"You can't tell. You have to promise."

"Just give me a clue then."

"I heard something when Dad and Nan thought I was asleep. Nan always gets us to bed so she can have her drinks. She thinks I don't know, like a kid or something. But I heard her and Dad talking. You have to promise not to tell."

"This is awfully hard for me, Matthew."

"I just wanted to discuss it with you. See what you think."

"Matthew, was your father with Gracie that afternoon when we were at the lodge?" I could tell from his face that I was right. "Matthew, I'm sure your father didn't do anything to Gracie."

"Nan said they'd pin it on him because they'd rather he did it than Steven."

"Matthew, that's ridiculous. Look, if your dad was there he'll have to tell the police. It would narrow down the time, too, so they can find the real person who tried to kill her."

Matthew didn't answer me.

"I'll tell you what, Matthew. I'll talk to your father."

"No! I'm not supposed to know. He also told Nan that Gracie said Mom wanted to go back with him, but I don't think that's true at all."

"I don't think so either, Matthew."

"He told Nan that Gracie kissed him. I never liked that Gracie." He shook his head. "Remember the day last summer when her letter came?"

"Yes, and we should have thrown it right into the garbage! Come on, let's go out to your dad's place. I'll tell him I heard a rumour that he was around Marion's place, that someone saw his truck there."

"But no one saw his truck. She said to park downtown and walk. That's what he told Nan. They'd notice his truck, but no one walks in Meredith in the winter if they can help it."

"Someone could have seen him. That's what I'll tell your father. Don't look at me like that. It's not really a lie. I did hear a rumour. From you."

"You won't tell the cops?"

"No, I won't. I'll try to persuade your father to tell them himself. They'll find his fingerprints anyway. They dusted for prints."

"But Dad's prints aren't on file! He's never been arrested!"

"Matthew, someone could have really seen him. How will it look if the police find out he was there and he didn't come forward? That's when he'll really be in trouble."

"You won't say I told you?"

"I promise."

I dropped Matthew off at the side of the road so he could pretend he had been checking rabbit snares.

I don't think I have ever been in Gladdie's house when the television wasn't on. Today it was blaring away with her soaps, and Timmy and Jody were parked two feet away from the screen. Gladdie's feet in pink slippers were up on the recliner and the room was filled with cigarette smoke.

"Jesus, what about that Limey doctor, aye?" She was obviously delighted at the news about Steven. "That sure was something that happened to that friend of yours."

I sat on the couch.

"You come for the kids? Matthew's out in the woods checking his father's snares. I hate to say it, but I feel for Allison, it all turning out this way."

I bet you do, I thought. There was a grin on Gladdie's face.

"Actually, I came to tell Matthew that the book he wanted is in at the library," I lied.

Gladdie snorted. "All this reading's not healthy. At least out here he gets some fresh air. I keep telling him he'll ruin his eyes if he don't keep his nose out of a book. I don't know where he gets it from."

"I've heard they have more than one suspect," I told Gladdie. She frowned. "There's no reason to believe that Steven did it."

Joe, rumpled and red-eyed, appeared in the doorway.

"I thought that was your car," he told me.

"She come out to tell Matthew about this book. But he's out checking the snares."

"I'll put the kettle on," Joe said.

I followed him to the kitchen, but Gladdie, lugging her ashtray, was right behind. She shoved over a pile of Christmas cards and cutlery and plunked the ashtray on the table.

"I was telling your mother that rumour has it that the police have more than one suspect for Gracie's attempted murder."

"Just put the bags in a cup," Gladdie said. "'Course that Limey doctor did it."

Joe poured boiling water into the teapot.

"They say that woman had the hots for the doctor," Gladdie went on. "That's what I heard, anyways. The kids said she went out with him Christmas Eve. I bet Allison was fit to be tied.

"Go on," she told Timmy and Jody, who were rummaging in the fridge. "This is grown-up talk."

The boys ignored her. Joe tossed them each a can of Diet Pepsi and poured out the tea.

"I should really get going," I said. "Wish I could have seen Matthew, though. He's been waiting for that book."

"Let's see if we can find him," Joe said.

The tea was forgotten.

"Let's sit in my car," I said outside. "I really came to see you, Joe. I didn't want to upset your mother."

"I thought it was something like that. Mind if I smoke?"

"I'll just roll the window down."

He lit his cigarette.

"What I wanted to tell you was that I heard someone saw you outside Marion and Hugh's that afternoon."

"Oh, and who would that be now?"

"You know how Meredith is. A rumour. Were you there while we were at the lodge, Joe?"

"Yeah," he said after a moment. "Yeah, I was there. But I swear I didn't do anything to her."

"I believe that. You were as shocked as anyone when you delivered the boys. You even gave her mouth-to-mouth."

"Shit." He threw his cigarette butt out of the window. Lit another. "Shit, shit."

"You should tell the police, Joe."

"Yeah. Maybe I will. I'll think about it."

"I'd do more than think about it if I were in your shoes."

He shrugged.

"So what happened? Do you want to talk about it?"

"Hell, she phoned me that afternoon. I knew who she was because of the kids. The boys let a few things slip. I don't like to ask too many questions about what their mother's up to. My mother does enough of that for the two of us. So this Grace says she has something real important to tell me about Allison. That I should come over there and have a chat, how she's heard so much about me from the boys and would like to meet me.

"I should have told her where to stick it, but to tell you the truth, I was feeling kind of low about Allison getting engaged and all. So I told my mother and the kids this guy wanted to see me about buying my truck. Well, I had been talking about selling it.

"'Park downtown,' Grace says. She doesn't want Allison to know she was getting involved. Okay, I do that, and when I get there she has the Christmas lights on and music playing, 'Silent Night,' and stuff. We have a couple of drinks and before I know it I'm telling her about myself and Allison, real personal stuff. Gracie is crying and holding my hand. We have another drink and she says, 'I bet I know what you're thinking about. You're thinking about all the Christmases together as a family, aren't you? The kids up at six for Santa and all of you sitting there among the wrapping paper and toys.'

"She's a witch, I tell you, Carolyn. A real witch. That was

exactly what I was thinking. Soon I was bawling like a kid, the way Jody cried when his cat got run over. Okay, I had a fair amount to drink and I guess that had a lot to do with it.

"Then Grace says, 'I think you can have your family back together.' Says that Allison still cares about me and that she was disappointed about what happened in the summer."

"What happened in the summer?" I asked.

"It was Timmy's birthday. Marion was going to have the party at her place, but she had the house filled with those tourists of hers and Allison held the party at her house. I was never there before, at the townhouse. After the party kids went home, we had a few beers for old time's sake, just being friendly, and it got late and Allison said I could sleep in the rec room.

"But I couldn't sleep. It was so strange, me down there and her upstairs and us having been together so long. It was like the divorce was just a piece of paper, you know? I could hear her roaming around upstairs and then I heard her opening the fridge. So I joined her in the kitchen and we each had another beer.

"I don't know how it happened, but suddenly we were kissing— hell, we were together since we were kids. She was nineteen and I was twenty-one when we got married. So we were kissing and I had my arms around her. But then Allison said, 'No! No!' and ran upstairs.

"Grace says Allison was only waiting for me to go after her, and I got to admit the thought did occur to me, but I heard her bedroom door shut and I wasn't about to force myself on her. I've done a lot of things in my time, but rape's not one of them.

"And then Grace kisses me. Hell! That's the last thing I was expecting, and who knows where that would have led if the phone hadn't have rung."

"The phone rang?"

"Yup, and before I knew it Grace was handing me my coat and wishing me the best. Pretty slick, I tell you."

"Joe, you really have to tell the cops. It's better if you come forward. They dusted for prints. They'll discover you were there."

I saw Matthew walking into the yard. He gave me an anxious look, but Joe didn't notice.

"You don't think Gracie was telling the truth, do you?" he asked me. "About Allison wanting to get back together?"

"I doubt it, Joe."

"That's what I think, too. That Grace is a witch."

## Chapter Eight

We moved back to Marion's that evening. Linda said we were welcome to stay longer at the lodge, but she had her hands full with the brassy tourists from New York, a Mr. and Mrs. Nickel, who expected room service (including breakfast in bed) and were already complaining that there was no evening entertainment, not even a lowly pianist.

Marion and I tidied, while Hugh went to collect the kids, Peter took Conrad for a run, and Allison, slumped on the couch, continued to have hysterics about Steven.

Allison finally left a message on Sandra MacLeod's answering machine. "This is urgent, a matter of life and death," she said, identifying herself and leaving a phone number.

"I'm glad Allison called Sandra," I told Marion as we washed dishes. "She has to find out the truth sooner or later."

"I'm hoping you'll try to see this Sandra if you go south with Gracie," Marion said.

"Me?"

"Just so we know what we are dealing with here."

"Marion, you don't really suspect Steven had anything to do with Gracie, do you?"

"He's been lovely to all of us. But as they say in England, he 'keeps himself to himself.' He's a rather private person."

"So you do suspect something."

"Why would he run away?" Marion asked.


They airlifted Gracie in the morning and I drove to Hamilton. We had planned to attend the New Year's Eve bash at the lodge and return home the next day, a holiday made possible by Peter's new, super-capable assistant, Kenneth (who had been a publisher and gone broke), but Peter only went through the motions of saying he should accompany me to Hamilton.

Peter had gone out to rent videos for the boys the night before and encountered Oskar Lutz, home from Vancouver. Oskar, "the other Meredith nerd," as Peter called him, had been Peter's best, and only real, friend all through school, and I knew he was hoping to spend time with his old pal.

It wasn't snowing and the roads were clear, I told Peter. "And unless a disaster happens, I'll be back for New Year's Eve."

"Don't have a red-hot affair with you-know-who," Peter whispered in my ear as he kissed me goodbye.


Hamilton, on the banks of Lake Ontario in southern Ontario, is known as the Steel City. And for its pollution. In the summer you can often see a haze of smog hanging over its factories and apartment buildings. It sits on the side of a mountain, a pretty place, but the downtown is scarred and old.

A light snow was falling by the time I turned off Highway 401. McMaster Hospital is right next to the campus of McMaster University in the western part of the city. Westdale used to be a working-class neighbourhood, but like so many such places in southern Ontario, including our own Lancaster Street in Guelph, the brick houses and treed streets are now trendy. Boutiques and bistros line King Street. I gave a reading once in a cafe there.

As I turned into the hospital carpark, I wished nothing more than to have a cup of cappuccino on King Street and to browse in the stores. Or to drive home to Guelph, which was only a half hour away on the 401.

But I was already heading for Intensive Care. There was no police guard at the door of Gracie's room, but Gracie wasn't there. She had withstood the trip without worsening, I learned, but was having a CAT scan. It would take an hour.

I took the car out and headed for King Street, where I browsed in the Bryan Prince Bookseller store— I had been there before— with its shelves that reached to the high ceiling. Two of my mysteries were in stock and I autographed those and bought two Gail Bowen paperbacks to reread before driving a few blocks to a cafe, where a strong coffee and a bagel revived me.

I was tempted to drive home. What if I did abandon Gracie? She had caused me, and everyone else, nothing but trouble, I thought as I picked up a *Toronto Star* left on the next table. The front page news was about a massive snow storm in western Canada and a plane highjacking in the Middle East, but inside, on the Ontario page, I read:

## Doctor Sought for Questioning

**Meredith, Ontario. An American woman is in critical condition in hospital and remains unconscious following a head injury sustained on Boxing Day in this small community near North Bay. The woman's identity is being withheld pending notification of next-of-kin.**

**Dr. Steven MacLeod of Meredith is believed to have seen the woman shortly before other residents of the bed-and-breakfast establishment returned from an outing.**

**Dr. MacLeod was last seen on the early afternoon of December 26th.**

**Dr. MacLeod is described as being white, 38 years of age, five feet ten inches tall, 150 pounds, with light brown hair and blue eyes. He speaks with a Scottish accent.**

**Anyone knowing the whereabouts of Dr. MacLeod is asked to contact the nearest detachment of the Ontario Provincial Police.**

Above was a small photo, a head and shoulder shot, that showed Steven squinting into the sun. The corner of a woman's sweater appeared in the corner.

I recognized Allison's sweater. The picture had been taken on Marion and Hugh's patio at Thanksgiving.

Gracie had been returned to Intensive Care when I got back to the hospital. And there was a message for me from Neil Andersen.

He had seen the newspaper and called Marion, who told Neil where I was.

"So you know all about it," I said.

"How is she?"

"The same. They just did a CAT scan. What a mess." I was using the telephone at the nurses' station. A nurse was filling in forms, but she paid no attention. "I wish I'd never invited her. I don't know how much Marion told you."

"A lot. And then I spoke to Allison, who was pretty hysterical." He'd met Allison during her short stay in Guelph. "Can't say as I blame her, with that doctor taking off. Damn fool thing to do, if you ask me. Want me to come to the hospital?"

"You don't have to. Can't you keep away from police work?" Now the nurse did look up. "How was Christmas, by the way?"

"Like Christmas every year, except Maureen has her boyfriend living in now. Never mind police work. You shouldn't be there alone. Marion said Peter is staying in the great white north."

"He met an old friend. You really don't have to come to Hamilton, Neil."

But my voice must have conveyed little conviction, because Neil said he'd be there in forty-five minutes.


I was glad Neil was coming, I decided as I sat beside Gracie's bed. At the same time, I wished Peter had driven down with me. Peter and his red-hot affair! He could not have been too worried. But if Peter were with me, things might have been awkward after Gracie's revelation to him.

Intensive Care here was more austere than the hospital room in Meredith with its cheery little Christmas tree. I could see an old comatose man behind half-drawn curtains in the next bed. His rasping breath provided background music to Gracie's more even breathing.

She seemed stiller, more quiet than in Meredith, and as I sat there, once again old feelings of affection came back, even if she had blurted secrets and gone through my purse. She seemed so innocent. Her face looked thinner, as if she had lost weight. Fragile, almost. Her hair needed washing, and the short hospital gown sleeves revealed tell-tale marks in the crook of her left elbow.

She made me think about Joe. I wondered if he had contacted the police. If he'd seen the newspaper or heard something about Steven on television, he would wonder if I had been bluffing about there being rumours...

I had dozed off in the chair by the time Neil arrived, and I saw that the old man had company, too, a heavy-set older woman and a younger one in a bright purple parka.

"Hi, Carolyn." Neil's eyes crinkled in that way of his— it was the first thing I'd ever noticed about him when I met him following the death of George Austin-Wright. Austin-Wright had known Anna Anderson, who claimed to be Anastasia.

Neil gripped my shoulder.

"I must have fallen asleep."

"Nah, you were just closing your eyes for a minute. So this is your friend." There was no extra chair and he stood over Gracie's bed and stared at her.

"She looks so different. You should see her with her make-up on." What a dumb thing to say, I thought. "She's been unconscious for two-and-a-half days. Did Marion give you the details about—" I lowered my voice— "the morphine?"

Neil nodded. At least she wasn't on heroin, he said, or crack. But morphine was bad.

"I never would have believed she was an addict," I whispered.

"She could have become addicted after some medical problem," Neil said sensibly.

"Let me see if I can find you a chair. Or use mine. I need to stand up, get the circulation moving."

"Tell you what. Let's grab a coffee in the cafeteria. You can't stay here all the time."

It felt good to get out of Intensive Care. The cafeteria was bright, crowded with nurses and doctors, patients in bathrobes, and visitors. The snow was falling more thickly outside, and with the Christmas ornaments it was almost cheerful.

For a while we talked about Christmas. Neil had been prepared to dislike his daughter's boyfriend, but liked him after all; Santa had brought shirts, ties and a book on birds and binoculars. "They obviously think the old codger needs a hobby."

We had another coffee.

"I just can't believe Gracie will die," I said.

"She's in the best place possible," Neil said. "If they can do anything, they'll do it here. But I gather it's complicated. Do you think Allison's doctor friend did it?"

I shook my head. "And Allison's fiance. At least for the time being."

I wondered if I should tell Neil about Joe. But Neil would probably have felt he had to report this information. I decided to leave it alone.

"Tell me about Gracie."

"Well, you heard a lot more about her from Marion. You know about the letter Gracie sent me and that we talked on the phone." Neil nodded. I'd told him a bit about Gracie. "Her father, Reg, and my mother dropped her off at my grandmother's in Maine when I was twelve. She was a brassy, a street-smart kid then, brought up by her boozing father. But she was appealing and funny. I mentioned the nun business, didn't I? She had to go into a foster home and later she was adopted.

"She talked about that in Meredith, how she was a lot of trouble for her adoptive parents and then her new grandmother came for a visit and taught Gracie to knit. That changed her, she said. After that, she behaved. She had a good relationship with this grandmother and went to be with her when the old woman was ill. She's had a few relationships, but she says her real father, who found her again and wanted money from her, turned her off marriage. She was in therapy, she says. She became a teacher, and I really don't know much more than that except she has this knack, this ability, to get people to tell her things. People take to her, but she sort of overdoes it. She brought all these very expensive presents for everyone, insisted on cooking the meal Christmas Eve."

"What about all those phone calls? What did you talk about?"

"Oh, books we liked. Movies we'd seen. Vacations. She's been to Europe and to Hawaii. Clothes. My books. My writing. Dogs. She was really interested in my writing. She said she found a few of my earlier mysteries in libraries. We talked about life. You know, what's important, that kind of stuff. For a while, in November, we were talking almost every day."

"Who did the calling?"

"She called mostly. She had this alternate phone plan or something. It was cheaper for her to call, she said. She called in the evening, usually around nine. After she had her students' assignments marked and I was through writing for the day."

"Hmm. Where did she teach?"

"At some private school. She never told me the name. I was going to call you, actually. The library in Meredith was going to get information for me about private schools in the Chicago area, but they didn't get back to me. I guess they're understaffed. I wanted you to look in the Guelph Library for me." I thought of the reason I hadn't called. "But with being at the hospital all the time..." I shrugged. "Who would have thought that someone would want to kill her?"

"Trouble seems to follow people like your Gracie around. Their lives become entangled. A big drama."

"People like Gracie? What do you mean?"

"You say people tell her things. She must have had trouble before. Marion said she finagled going with that doctor on Christmas Eve. That kind of thing. And if she's been on morphine she must have had plenty of dramas and crises. Unless she had a very friendly doctor in Chicago."

"I don't know. Maybe she wanted to get her hooks into Steven so he would get her morphine."

"Doesn't it strike you as odd that in her story about her adoption, a grandmother played a pretty big role?"

"What are you saying?"

"You had a doting grandmother, so she had to have one, too."

"Mine didn't knit, though. She hated needlework. My grandmother read books and listened to the opera on the radio."

"But Marion knits. Marion is a big-time knitter."

"Go on."

"Maybe Gracie tells people what they want to hear, to

ingratiate herself. That's not a person who's had a secure life. Maybe she's not a teacher. Maybe she wasn't adopted."

"Allison didn't believe Gracie was a teacher, come to think of it. The adults got these fantastic gifts, but she gave the boys cheap paint-by-number kits... The kids didn't take to her at all and she didn't pay much attention to them either. Marion was suspicious, too."

"Remember Anna Anderson? She re-invented herself. Maybe Gracie has recreated herself, too. She could be almost anything. Or anyone."

"What do you mean?"

"Maybe she did a lot of research on you and found you once had this friend in Maine. You said on *Good Morning America* that you grew up in Maine. I think you named the town, too. So this woman's name is Grace and she assumes that other identity."

"That's dumb. I recognized Gracie from before."

"It's a long time ago. Did Gracie ever have her picture in the paper in Maine?"

"Come to think of it, she did. She won the potato sack race at a church picnic."

A smile spread on Neil's face.

"She could be a celebrity follower," he said. "She could be a journalist. A blackmailer."

"I think she's just a needy, mixed-up, annoying woman who can be immensely likeable," I said.

"You're probably right. But first thing tomorrow, I'll call this old buddy in the States— works as a private eye now— see what he can come up with."

"He's in Chicago?"

"No, in Michigan. But he'll know someone."

"I'm sure the police have checked."

"Let's see what we can find out, anyway."

"There was ID in her purse, Neil."

"Which, if it had her current address, should have led to locating her family. The landlord or neighbours would have known something. Credit unions, banks— she would have used a bank to pay rent— they would have been checked. The bank would have known where she worked. But presumably that's all been tried."

"She went through my purse," I told Neil, "and read a letter."

"Not nice."

"But not a criminal act. It wasn't an important letter, just a 'thank you' for visiting a school. But still... I think she's Gracie. What you're saying is just so weird."

"I am a cop, kiddo."

A clergyman was with the old man when we returned to Intensive Care and members of the family were congregated in the hall. "...still a shock," a woman's voice said. "At his age, it's all for the best," I heard. This was followed by the professionally reassuring voice of the pastor, who began to recite the twenty-third Psalm.

"The Lord is my shepherd..."

Gracie's face twitched. I took her hand and Neil stood by the bed while the familiar words filled the room. What if Neil's speculations and Marion's suspicions were true? What if this woman wasn't Gracie? I thought of Anna Anderson and the aristocratic followers who believed she was Anastasia, the youngest daughter of the Tsar of Russia. Ten years after Anderson's death, DNA tests confirmed she was really a Polish-German woman named Franziska. What if the tests had been done while she was alive? Would her followers have deserted her? Would she have been re-united with her peasant family?

What if Gracie did turn out to be someone else? She would still be the woman I'd chatted with for months over the telephone...

There it was again: Gracie's innate ability to create belief and sympathy, I thought, as I watched her face and squeezed her hand.

Suddenly she opened her eyes and stared at me.

"Gracie?"

Her eyes widened and bulged. Her hand clamped mine.

"Gracie! You're in the hospital. Everything's going to be all right! It's me, Carolyn!"

My voice must have risen because there was silence behind the curtain by the old man's bed.

Gracie's eyes closed and her hand fell limp.

"I'm sure she recognized me, Neil. She did, I know she did. I should tell the nurse. Maybe she's starting to come around."

The curtain parted as I went past and the clergyman's face peered out. It was a cherubic face topped with slicked-back black hair and he smiled at me.

"Thanks for the psalm," I told him. "I think my friend heard, because she opened her eyes."

The family members looked startled, as if I had no business addressing their minister.

A nurse came to check on Gracie, but Gracie slept on. It often happened, the nurse said, that comatose patients opened their eyes. It didn't mean much, she added, as she checked Gracie's IV drip. "But we can hope."

"I'm going to spend the night here," I told Neil. "Just in case Gracie wakes up."

"I'll stay too, then. But you're going to be exhausted."

"There's a couch in the lounge. I can have a nap there. You don't have to stay, Neil."

"I will if you want me to."

I shook my head. Neil looked relieved. Maybe he was anxious to call his Michigan friend.

"Neil— hold off on calling your friend, okay?"

He raised an eyebrow.

"It just seems so awful to be doing that at this point," I explained. "Let's see if she comes to. If she doesn't, well, you can still phone, of course."

"It's your decision, Carolyn. I won't do anything you don't want me to do."

"I'm just going to sit with her and tell myself she is the Gracie I knew. For now, anyway. If you have time, you could check the phone directory in the library for private schools in Chicago."

"Sure thing. Do you want to have dinner first?"

I shook my head. "I'll grab something in the cafeteria."

"Tell you what. I'll be back in the morning unless I hear differently. And tomorrow night we'll have dinner. How's that?"

"Fantastic. Now get out of here before you have me believing Gracie is really Jane Doe."

Before he left, Neil told me that the pastor, a Reverend Browning, had recognized me. He was a real fan, Neil said.

The night passed in a boring, uneventful way. I ate lasagna in the cafeteria and tried to read my Gail Bowen, but couldn't focus. There was no change in Gracie. I dozed on a vinyl couch in the lounge and leafed through old *Time* magazines.

At eight-thirty I left a message on Neil's machine that I was leaving the hospital. I drove home in a sleepy daze and wanted only to shower and sleep for a few hours in my own bed, but that turned out to be impossible.

Someone had broken into our house.

# Chapter Nine

The only damage was a broken pottery vase in the living room. Nothing had been taken, but someone had gone through the closets and cupboards. Cereal boxes and pasta packages were dumped on the kitchen floor and most of our clothes were tossed on the bed. We hadn't stopped the mail and late Christmas cards and circulars, along with a letter from my publisher, Jake Hendricks, about some planned readings, littered the hooked rug in the living room.

The computer, television, VCR and CD player were untouched.

"You have to call the police," Neil said.

"I did. I called you."

"You know what I mean. The city of Guelph isn't OPP jurisdiction."

"You think this has something to do with Gracie, don't you?"

"Sure do. Someone wants her dead. Someone breaks into your place, doesn't take a damn thing."

"But I don't have anything of hers. Except the letters, and they're still here."

"They could have thought she sent something to you."

"Drugs?"

"Sure. Say she wanted to get drugs across the border. Maybe to sell to another party. So she sends you a package."

"You forget Gracie was going to fly out of the Soo on New Year's Day."

"Was she? She sounds pretty persuasive. It would have been easy for her to twist your arm, talk you into an extended visit. Says how much she wants to see your house. Next thing you know you're inviting her to come south with you. The package is there. Maybe she addressed it to herself, a Christmas gift for you. Naturally you let her open it as it's addressed to her. Inside is something for you, a tablecloth, say, but there's something else."

"Hmm."

"Or she tells someone she's sent the parcel to your house and then this person breaks in."

"That's awful. You mean she wanted this person to break in while we were away?"

"Maybe. She knew you'd be up north."

"But she didn't know we didn't have the mail stopped. And if she had sent this lethal package, why did they go through everything?"

"Don't forget our Canadian postal system. Maybe the parcel's late and the culprits will be back."

"Why leave everything in a mess then?"

"Because you're not expected back until New Year's Day is why."

"There's only one thing wrong with your theory, Neil. Okay, say this package was supposed to be here. It would have been with the mail. I wouldn't have hidden it because I wasn't here to hide it!"

"Unless it came early..."

"Then I would have taken it to Meredith with all the other

Christmas presents. And how would this person— whoever broke in— have known we hadn't asked someone to water the plants?"

"You did. You asked me to check, if I remember correctly, and like a true and faithful friend I was here yesterday and watered your poinsettias and that big tree thing, and not a thing was touched. But, wait. They panic. They think you might have come here to clean up, check the mail, whatever, before you head for the hospital in Hamilton. So this idiot panics. You've hidden the drugs."

Neil beamed at me.

"One thing is for sure, you can't stay here. You can bunk at my place. We'll call the cops, they'll set up a stake-out, and you'll be cosy and safe in my suburban palace."

The phone rang before I could answer.

There was no one there. After a moment there was a click. I shivered.

"Looks like someone's checking if there's anyone here," I told Neil.

"Now will you call the police? You have to, you know. And you definitely cannot stay here."

"I can't stay at your place, Neil, and I'm going to tell you why."

We were both embarrassed after I repeated to Neil what I had foolishly told Gracie.

"Peter will hit the roof if I stay with you."

"Yeah, I can see that. That Gracie is a dangerous woman, Carolyn."

"I can go to a hotel," I said.

"After you call the police," Neil said.

I shook my head.

"It's stupid, but Gracie could be in enough trouble as it is."

"You want to tamper with evidence? What if a parcel of dope arrives?"

"I don't know what I'd do, Neil."

"You'd be a fool not to turn it over to the police. An even bigger fool to hold on to it or destroy it. They'll be after you. These druggies don't care what they do. This shipment could be worth thousands. I don't like any of this, Carolyn. And you can't stay here. You don't even have Conrad to protect you."

"Why wouldn't Gracie have mailed this mythical parcel to Meredith?"

"Because it would be connected to her, that's why. And Meredith is such a small place. Don't forget that."

"An out-of-the-way place, too. Gracie could have arranged for a pick-up. She would have thought of something up there. Developed a sudden passion to learn all about rabbit snares, for instance."

"Are you going to call the police?"

"You really think I should?"

"What have I been talking about?"

"You're right. I know you're right."

Two Guelph police officers came to the house, and inspected the "damage," but they said they could do little. For one thing, there had been similar break-ins along Lancaster Street yesterday and the police were keeping an extra watch on the neighbourhood.

All of the break-ins had been at empty houses, the police said. In one house an expensive wrist-watch had been stolen, but mainly the houses had been messed up.

"So that is that," I told Neil. "I might as well clean up the mess and put everything back."

"I'll give you a hand. Tell you what, I'll stay here and you go to a hotel. That way the house won't be empty and you'll be safe at the same time."

And Peter won't have anything to complain about, I thought, as I straightened the bedroom closet, while Neil tidied the living room where the police had dusted for prints. Would this be the end of our friendship? I wondered. My confession to Gracie, my loose talk, and her revelations, her lies to Peter, had changed things. And now Neil knew. How would Neil feel? Would he stop dropping in? He might think it was better to break off our friendship than to let it develop into something that would mean trouble and heartache.

Or— what if I had made a fool of myself? Neil might only have seen me as a friend.

I would miss his presence in my life if I lost him, I realized.

After everything was put back to rights, Neil and I had a cup of tea in the living room. It was Neil who suggested tea, not a drink.

"I put all your mail on the hall table," Neil said. "You don't mind me staying here, do you? Because I still think there's more to this than meets the eye. What if there had been a parcel and whoever broke in thought it went to the wrong address? All the Christmas mail, mistakes happen."

"I don't mind."

"I could park my car around the corner and not answer the phone, let the machine get it."

"You mean, Peter... This is dumb. Of course I'll tell Peter."

We were silent. I drank my tea. The living room was tidy now, and we had put up a little tree for the weeks before we left for Meredith, but my familiar room with its pine furniture and books seemed dreary. The heat was still turned down and I hadn't had a shower or a rest.

"If I'm staying in a hotel anyway, I might as well stay in Hamilton to be closer to the hospital."

Neil nodded.

"Neil, I..." I could feel my face turning red.

"You feel like an idiot," he completed for me.

"I shouldn't have opened my big mouth to Gracie. It was just wine talk. I mean, I... I don't know what I mean. This is nuts."

"Don't worry about it, Carolyn. I know what it's like to spill your guts at two in the morning."

"I wasn't really spilling my guts..."

"Oh, I know that, kiddo. I'm not exactly Adonis."

"I didn't mean that. I should throw a few things together for the hotel..."

But I didn't get up.

"I just don't want this to ruin our friendship," I said.

Neil nodded. He looked uncomfortable and picked up the remote control for the television. But the TV was hidden in the Dutch cupboard and he put the remote back on the table.

"You'd miss the doughnuts," Neil said. He often picked up a few from Tim Horton's on his way to see us. "What are off-duty cops for except to run into doughnut shops?"

"Can we please forget the whole mess?"

"And keep those doughnuts coming?"

"And keep those doughnuts coming."


Neil walked me to the door fifteen minutes later. He waited while I put my boots on.

"Well..." I straightened up.

"We'll forget it," Neil said. "Don't worry about it."

He smiled at me in that Neil-like way, with his eyes crinkling up.

"You're pretty nice yourself, you know," he said.

And then he gave me a hug. We had never hugged before, or touched, the way friends do. He held me tightly for a minute, and our hands and lips just brushed. Then he released me.

"I'd better get out of here, if you ever want to see another doughnut in your life."

He didn't say anything about joining me in Hamilton the next day.

## Chapter Ten

The Holiday Inn in downtown Hamilton certainly wasn't home, but it felt good to shower and rest in the anonymous, immaculately clean hotel room. I called the hospital, learned there was no change, and told them where I could be reached before falling into a deep and dreamless sleep.

Neil's hug: we were attracted to each other. We would remain friends. I thought of Peter and knew I didn't want to jeopardize our marriage. But the *idea* of Neil was there.

I awoke at nine the next morning and called Meredith quickly. Peter was out with Oskar, Marion told me, and there was still no word from Steven. Allison had been phoning Sandra MacLeod all day, but only reached the machine.

"The more she telephones, the more frantic Allison gets,"

Marion told me. "Sandra's probably away over the Christmas holidays."

She'd give Peter the news about the break-in, Marion told me.

"The rumours are flying around Meredith," Marion said. "According to Joe, the story has it that your friend Grace is really a high-priced prostitute."

"According to Joe???"

"Yes, I know. He was here for a couple of hours this afternoon. It is strange. He offered to take the boys for the afternoon, but he spent most of the time with Allison. If only Steven would turn up! There has to be a logical explanation for his disappearance! I'm so afraid Allison will turn to Joe out of desperation."

So Joe hadn't gone to the police, I thought as Marion went on about Joe and Allison.

"If you could try to find out something about this Sandra person... I know you have your hands full, but perhaps if you tried calling it might make a difference. Maybe Sandra is there and just doesn't want to talk to Allison."

"Give me the number," I said. "I'll try calling later tonight."

It was almost ten by the time I returned to the hospital, and the old man was dying. They had moved him to a private room, but I recognized the relatives clustering around the lobby, talking in quiet, serious voices.

Gracie was alone in Intensive Care. Sleeping on and on. There was a smaller bandage on her head, but otherwise she looked the same. I sat by her bed for half an hour and went in search of a coffee. I'd need coffee to get through the night, I decided.

The woman in the purple parka was at the vending machine and nodded at me. We carried our styrofoam cups back to the Intensive Care unit together.

"How is your sister?" she asked inquisitively. Some of her coffee spilled on the floor and she rubbed it with her boot. She had a round face that would normally be complaisant, but now it was alive. I understood this: they had kept a vigil for a long time and now, at last, something was happening.

"She's my friend," I said, and before I knew it I was explaining my relationship to Gracie.

"Maine? You don't say. I thought she'd be your sister. They don't generally let anyone but close family into Intensive Care. I had this friend once, she lived with a guy for eight years, and she had trouble getting in. He was in this car accident, see, and first they didn't think he'd make it. Drunken driver. I'm telling you. Every time I read in the paper that someone got off with nothing but a fine I could hit the roof. He was only thirty-two, my friend's boyfriend. Of course, when someone's as old as my grandfather, as Pop, it's different. But it's still a shock."

Pop, of course, was who she wanted to talk about. He was ninety-one "going on twenty-five" and had been revived twice since his coronary. This time there was too much brain damage, the doctors said, and the family had decided to have the machine turned off, I learned as I settled in the lounge with the woman and a man wearing a suit.

They were Erna and Mason, I learned, and Erna repeated Gracie's story to her brother.

"But you hear of people coming back out of comas," Erna said. "You read about it in magazines. This friend of mine, she had an appendix operation and something went wrong with the anaesthetic and they almost lost her. Had to revive her and she remembered everything, so you never can tell. Your friend might pull out of it."

Mason wrung his hands.

"You never know," he said as the minister came in.

Reverend Browning, the pastor from Pop's church.

"Robert Browning," he said as he shook my hand. "I'm glad to make your acquaintance, Ms. Archer. It's long been an ambition of mine to put pen to paper, or turn on the computer as it were."

"Computers." Erna rolled her eyes.

"Of course I couldn't hope to match your standards. I'm quite the mystery reader myself."

The pastor looked like he wanted to continue talking to me, but the family members were waiting for him to pray by the bedside and— reluctantly, I must admit— I returned to Gracie's room.

Where, once again, I fell asleep in the chair. And awoke sometime later to find the pastor standing by Gracie's bed. I looked at him inquiringly. He nodded. The old man had died half an hour ago, he said.

"Do you mind?" He indicated en empty chair across the room, carried it over, and settled himself comfortably. For a while we talked about Gracie. Erna had told him about my old friendship with Gracie, I thought, and he made the appropriate, sympathetic noises and even uttered a short prayer, but the topic he really wanted to discuss was writing. He didn't just have dreams of writing, he had actually written a mystery novel! Only he didn't like to tell church people about it.

It can be annoying when complete strangers approach me to discuss their work and aspirations, but I didn't mind this time. Robert Browning— what a name!— had certainly recovered from witnessing the death of his old parishioner— I supposed he was used to such things— and his face was alight with excitement.

He had never met a writer before! Could I believe it? Of course, in his line of work he met all kinds of people, and there were some ladies in his church who had a poetry circle, but he steered clear of them.

"The thing is, I feel sure I could sell my mystery. I've got the background down. They say in these writers' books that you should write about what you know and there's nothing I know better than churches. It's set in a church, not mine, more a compilation of churches I've pastored, and the organist is found dead just as a wedding is about to start. I made the assistant minister a woman, more timely, you know, with women's lib. But the sleuth will be the pastor, who's a regular guy. His wife hates being married to a minister, for instance, and the ladies in the church aren't exactly crazy about her. But the point is, what do you do when it's finished?"

I explained about query letters, agents and publishers.

"No one wants to read it, that's the trouble. I've even thought of paying someone to publish it. You wouldn't be interested in reading it, by chance? I know it's a lot to ask, but I feel Providence put you here. Oh, I know that sounds fatuous and it is a lot to ask... It's funny, but when I saw you on television I had this feeling we'd meet some time."

"And here we are," I said. "But I hardly think my friend here was bopped on the head so we could meet. And don't say that God moves in mysterious ways."

The man looked so wimpy with his boyish, angelic face. Not at all like a minister, I thought. I wondered if he wore that silly grin when he conducted funerals.

"I bet you have your novel with you," I said. I was beginning to feel a little crazy.

He did. It was in a ring binder; all wrong. And he had copies of letters he'd sent out enquiring if the editor ("Dear Sir or Madam") would be interested in reading "a sprightly and entertaining novel in the mystery genre."

"What if I lose it?"

"Not to worry. I have a copy at home, one in my bank vault, and another at my mother's house."

"No promises," I said.

"Meeting you has been my real Christmas present," he said as he walked— waddled with little steps— away.

Life can be surprising, and I was surprised that night. Soon I had forgotten about Gracie and fallen into the Reverend Browning's wonderful manuscript.

It was set in a fictional small town, Chapters, and featured the Reverend Willy Melrose and his nympho wife Rosie. Willy was the original nerd, a fat little mama's boy whose mother still ordered suits from Sears and Eaton's for him. Despite this, Willy was always dodging women, from his scatter-brained secretary, Harriet, to Rosie, who was always, morning, noon, and night, lying in wait for her hubby. Poor Willy really liked having tea with the Ladies' Aid. He wanted poached eggs for breakfast, not a naked wife trying to pull his zipper down. And he wanted, more than anything, to solve the mystery of the murder of the organist, a frizzy-haired artistic type called Emery Thatcher, who, it seemed, had been having affairs with many church women, including the preacher's nubile wife.

It was after two when I finished the manuscript. A good night's work, I told myself.

"I have just read the most crazy, wonderful mystery, Gracie. About a character like you, only he's a man. Someone who tries to get into everyone's good graces and goes overboard."

Did a smile flit across Gracie's face? I kissed her forehead and went to find a pay telephone.

It's not every publisher you can phone at two in the morning, but Jake was always telling me I was too conventional, and I had no compunction at all about calling this late at night. I've known him for ages, ever since my first cookbook came out.

Jake hated answering machines and his sleepy voice answered on the first ring. He made no reference to the time.

"Carolyn, love. Is Meredith driving you crazy yet?"

"I'm not in Meredith," I told him and filled him in on Gracie's disastrous visit to my in-laws'. I even told him about Joe. "But that's not why I'm calling. I've been sitting by Gracie's bedside and have just finished reading the most wonderful, crazy mystery manuscript by this preacher fellow who was hanging around."

"Hanging around, huh?"

"They do tend to hang around hospitals. An old man died tonight and this minister was here. One of my biggest fans, it turned out, and when he came back to the hospital he brought his manuscript with him. It's in this big ugly blue ring binder."

"A ring binder, huh?"

"He doesn't have two clues, but that doesn't matter. It's wonderful and I want you to read it."

"When can I expect this masterpiece?"

"Tomorrow. Unless Gracie takes a turn for the worse. Or the

better. Unless there's a change I'll see you tomorrow if you're in the office. I'll just go in and come right back to Hamilton."

"I'm always in the office. You know me. Waiting for masterpieces."

"Don't be smart. You won't regret reading this. How was Christmas?" I knew Jake and his brother always had Christmas dinner with an old aunt.

"Prim, prim." I heard Jake blowing his nose. "Maybe you'll cheer me up."

"If the manuscript cheered me up when I was sitting beside a comatose friend, it'll enrapture you, who've had nothing more traumatic than dinner with your old aunt."

"Who never serves anything but tomato juice," Jake said.

Back at the Holiday Inn, I tried Sandra MacLeod's number and got the answering machine. I identified myself as a writer and left the number of Hendricks Publishing.

I also called Neil. No one had come near our place, he said. He had nuked some chili from the freezer. ("At least the food's better than at my place. House-sitting has its compensations when you sit for Carolyn Archer...")

I told him about making a quick trip to Toronto the next day, but he did not offer to accompany me.

# Chapter Eleven

There was no change with Gracie, and it felt good to speed along the 401 to Toronto. I considered taking the GO train, but it's only a forty minute drive and I didn't want to be dependent on train schedules and subways, especially as I was carrying a bulky manuscript in a big ring binder.

Hendricks Publishing on Greenfield was cheery with Christmas decorations, but of the most tasteful kind. Hendricks Publishing is in an old brick house right downtown, and a real fir wreath with a red velvet bow hung on the oak door. A tiny tree adorned only with white lights and tinsel stood on the corner table which held various art magazines and literary catalogues. A plate of gingerbread men stood on the round table before the black leather sofa in the reception room.

All these Christmasy touches were, I knew, the work of Jake's assistant, Molly. Jake, left to his own devices, would probably have strung up coloured lights or simply not bothered.

Molly greeted me warmly. I've known her as long as I've known Jake and I have a lot to be grateful to her for, as she'd brought my first cookbook manuscript to Jake's attention. I hadn't seen her since September, and I was surprised that she'd let her hair go completely grey, but otherwise she was still the eccentric, hippie lady from the sixties with a dash of the church vicar's wife thrown in.

Jake, alas, was out with a "poet having a crisis."

"Christmas and crises go together like mistletoe and plum pudding," Molly said, wrinkling her nose. She used to share her house on the beaches with an assortment of young men, but she'd recently sold the place and was living alone now. "Let's have a coffee."

"Anyone I know having the post-Christmas breakdown?"

"Jonathon Frisco-Chaquin." Molly rolled her eyes as she poured out coffee from the carafe on her desk. "You probably met him at a launch. A guy with bitten-down nails? He's married to Jacqueline Esper, the poet, although we don't publish her. Anyway, she took off a while ago and Jonathon waited until Christmas to have his breakdown. He says his wife stole his last manuscript."

"So Jake's holding his hand."

"Helping to bend the elbow is more like it. Jake said you were bringing in a manuscript."

"A wonderful mystery. I'd leave it with you but I know he'll try to put off reading it."

"I could threaten to break his arm. Oh, by the way, Peter called."

"Peter? I didn't tell him I was coming here. He's still in Meredith."

"I thought he was calling from Guelph." Molly raised an eyebrow. "And there's another message. Let's see."

She shifted a pile of envelopes out of the way and threw them to the floor. "Sandra MacLeod. Said she wasn't doing any more interviews. You're not doing another cookbook, are you?" she asked suspiciously. Hendricks wanted me to keep writing mysteries, which made more money. Or rather, Molly wanted me to keep penning the whodunits.

"No, it's a personal thing. This Sandra MacLeod. I left Hendricks' number knowing I'd be in Toronto. She must have me confused with someone else. No more interviews? You haven't heard of her by any chance, have you?"

"Nope. You know what they say about five minutes of fame. You can use Jake's office to make your calls if you want."

I called Peter first. *Neil* had told him I would be in Toronto.

"I should have called you but it was so late last night when I decided to come here that I was afraid I'd wake everyone up."

"Did Neil go to Toronto with you?"

"Peter!!! Of course not. He's baby-sitting the house in case the bad guys come back. Neil thinks they were looking for something that Gracie sent us."

Peter was silent for a minute. "How is she?" he asked at last.

"The same. Exactly the same. I wouldn't have driven into Toronto if there'd been a change. Listen, Peter, Steven's ex-wife left a message for me at Hendricks. She seems to think I want to interview her for something or other, so apparently she does not want to talk to Allison. I'm going to try to talk to this Sandra today, but please tell Allison to stop calling her machine. How's everyone else? Your mother told me Joe's been hanging around."

"Hmm. Just our luck to have Allison back with him. He just called a few minutes ago and said the cops want to question him. He was very upset and is coming by Mom's on his way to the station."

"Oh, no."

"He said he wanted to talk to Allison first."

Should I tell Peter about Joe seeing Gracie that day? Would Joe let on that he had told me? I'd better be open with Peter, I decided, and told him what Joe had told me.

Again, there was a long silence.

"You didn't think you could confide in me?" he asked at last.

"I didn't tell anyone. I miss you, Peter. The house seemed

empty without you and Conrad there. How is the big goof, by the way?"

"Puking," Peter said. "Mom cooked a small turkey and he threw up entire pieces of breast meat. You could have washed them off and not known they'd ever been down his gullet. No one can figure out how he got them."

"But he's okay now?"

"Yeah. Did you tell Neil about Joe?"

"What is this?" I sighed and pushed away a stack of book catalogues. "You're being the green-eyed monster and I don't like it. There is absolutely nothing between Neil and me and you know it."

"It's all Gracie's fault," Peter said.

"It's my fault for talking like a teenager who's had too much to drink!"

Jake still had not come back by the time I was through talking to Peter. Why not use the time to try to see Sandra? I wondered. If she had phoned Hendricks, she could be home. It would do no good to telephone her again. She lived in Willowdale and it would be easier to go out by subway than to crawl along Yonge Street in the car. I would leave the manuscript with Molly and talk to Jake when I got back, I decided.

But I should have taken the car, I realized as soon as I got into the subway car. Not only did two women stare and stare at me (so many mystery readers are women), but an unshaven, dirty drunk began hassling me for money. His eyes looked glazed and I thought he was probably a mental patient, obviously disturbed.

I was glad I hadn't brought the manuscript along as he glanced at my purse. The two women starers looked away, obviously not wanting to get involved.

"Wanna go to my place? Wanna fuck? Wanna see the moon?"

I pretended not to hear, and changed seats.

"My own mother told me to get out of the house," he mumbled, moving to the seat behind mine. "Right over Christmas. I had no choice, no choice at all."

I moved to sit beside one of the women. She raised an eyebrow. I shrugged. Maybe I had been mistaken in thinking she and the other woman, who was getting to her feet, had recognized me. The world wasn't filled with fans after all.

The man began singing "Jingle Bells" and laughing. He was looking right at me. My stop was coming soon. If he followed me to the platform I'd inform security and have them send for the police, I decided.

At last my stop came. I went out the nearest door, and just as the train was pulling out, the maniac sprinted out as well. But he didn't follow me up the stairs. There were no footsteps behind me and when I looked back, he was standing and talking to himself.

According to the city map, it was only two blocks to Sandra MacLeod's place, but I decided to take a taxi to be safe.

The address turned out to be a highrise, and I was still shaking when I pressed the buzzer of apartment 704.

The voice that answered my ring had a faint Scottish accent to it.

"I am not interested in more interviews. I left a message to that effect."

"I don't want to interview you. This is a personal matter."

"Concerning?"

But I was sure that she knew.

"Look, I really want to see you. To talk to you. My sister-in-law has been leaving messages on your machine, I know, but I..." I fumbled for the right words. The episode on the subway had shaken me. We have our nutbars in Guelph, too, but I hadn't taken the subway in years. "I'm sorry. I had rather an unfortunate experience on the subway. I came directly from my publisher's office. Check with them if you like."

"No. I shall come downstairs and look you over. If you seem at all disreputable or dangerous or appear to be working for a tabloid I shall simply disappear!"

The woman who came out of the elevator five minutes later was fortyish, with strong features, no-nonsense short brown hair, and a tall, bony frame. We peered at each other through the glass door and I thought she was going to laugh, but her mouth remained stern. I fumbled in my handbag for ID, but she shook her head and at last she smiled, which quite transformed her face.

"I do think I have seen you on television," she said, shaking hands. "Mystery writer, are you not?"

"I wish I had a book with me so I could assure you that I do not work for a tabloid."

"Indigent writers have been known to do so, but I don't suppose you are indigent. Come upstairs then. You look safe enough. What's this about the subway?" she asked as the elevator doors slid open.

"Just a maniac following me. Some nut. I should have driven—

I left my car at Hendricks— but I thought the subway would be easier, with parking and so on."

"Good heavens, yes. I don't even own a car," she said as the elevator stopped on the seventh floor.

Her apartment was an odd mixture of typical white-walled highrise with a low-slung couch and unimaginative glass tables and a few old pieces, a desk with a big dictionary on the top, and a scarred bookcase filled, I saw, with historical novels. The only concession to Christmas was a gigantic poinsettia and a few cards displayed on top of the bookcase.

"Tea? Or perhaps something a bit stronger after your unfortunate experience?" She raised her eyebrows at the term 'unfortunate experience' as if she might be laughing at me. But if she was, it wasn't with meanness. Her eyes were twinkling. She probably carried a good, stout umbrella to ward off unwanted advances.

"Something stronger, I think."

"Good woman. Wise choice. I think I shall need something stronger myself, as I am quite certain you wish to discuss my misbegotten marriage."

She poured us each a generous inch of Scotch and settled herself with her glass on the chair opposite the couch.

"But first I must explain about the interview business," she said. "As they say, 'to make a long story short,' I saved a child from drowning in Lake Ontario last summer and have been hounded by the press ever since. The breath of life, you know? Any fool can do it. I would do it for any fool, which, it seems, I did. Ghastly family, ghastly. Ghastly child, come to that. I won't bore you with the details, but the grandmother, the matriarch, is a publicity hound. I have been invited to the child's birthday, to the mother's birthday, and each time the press appeared. Pull of the heart strings. Most lately, I was invited for Christmas dinner. I refused. That was another angle for Old Grandma to call the press. I am now refusing to have anything to do with the family. Grandma is a perfectly dreadful woman who likes to drink and cry. Her trucker husband left her for another woman two years ago and she felt he had been kidnapped and managed to appear on television, begging for the kidnappers to release her dear beloved. He turned up in Indiana a week later with the truck dispatcher from his office, but came back with his tail between his legs. Grandma wears sequins in her hair and offered to have my colours done and I wasn't going there to weep, wail and drink at Christmas. Cheers."

We drank.

"Well, I can understand your predicament," I said. "They do sound— ghastly." I stumbled over the last word, which my friend, Millicent Mulvey, had used frequently.

"But of course you are here to discuss Steven, who has gotten himself into a fine mess, according to his mother. Don't look so surprised. Steven and I are second cousins and I was his sister's best friend. Still am, although I only see her every few years."

"You haven't seen Steven?"

"No, and I have no yearning to do so. I managed to evade him on visits to Scotland, or perhaps it was vice versa. He had no great desire to see me, I am sure. His sister, Betty, didn't even write me that he had emigrated to Canada. I didn't learn he was in this country until his mother called me. She would never have done so had she not been that upset. Perhaps she thought Steven might contact me in his hour of need."

"You didn't read about it in the paper?"

"I only take the *Globe*. They don't concentrate on the seedy ordinary little crimes. I did not call his girlfriend back because she seemed like the weeping and wailing kind. Nor did I want to spoil Steven's chances, if it came to that. But tell me exactly why they are looking for him."

How many times had I told Gracie's story? I wondered, as I began. It was easiest to start with Maine, because that was the beginning that made all the rest possible. From Maine it was a jump to Gracie's reappearance in my life and then to Christmas, Steven's visit to Gracie, followed by his disappearance.

"But none of us think he would have tried to kill Gracie," I said. "He seemed to be the kindest, nicest man. Allison is crazy about him. The only adverse thing I've heard about Steven is that he can be a bit snobby, but they often say that about newcomers in Meredith, especially if they're educated and from Great Britain."

"Steven broke my arm," Sandra said.

"What?"

Sandra returned to the desk and took out the bottle, which she brought to the coffee table. She poured us each another bit of Scotch.

"Shocks you, does it? I did tell you I didn't want to harm Steven's chances with your sister-in-law. I agree with you that he's basically an honest and decent person, but he did break my arm. This is all so difficult to explain. I never talk about it, although it's no secret. The police weren't involved; we hushed it up."

I took a big sip.

"I don't understand why you wouldn't want to warn Allison, then."

"We were both young. Eighteen. I was a wild one, and Steven, well, Steven was the quiet little scholar. We eloped. I still don't understand it, except a fellow had jilted me and Steven was a cousin. Familiar, safe, on his way to the university. He had a scholarship. His mother had taken in sewing to help him along. We were crazy, both of us, Steven and I. He'd never had a girl— I mean sexually— and I'd had one too many boys. I was perfectly ghastly, grunging around in long skirts and spouting off about free love.

"So we eloped, went to Gretna Green, and there we were. No money. His mother almost had a heart attack, at first, but she tried to make the best of things and arranged a little reception for us in her parlour. I got drunk and persuaded Steven to drink. Had a bottle in my purse, kept telling him to be a man and a drunkard.

"I had a job in a fish-and-chip shop and Steven went to work at the dockyards. First we lived with his mother, but I was having none of that, and we set up housekeeping in a little flat right above the fish shop. They could hear us battling down there when I wasn't working. It became a joke. Steven and the missus at it again.

"We threw things, I ripped his trousers, he tossed my hair curlers out the window. We were both totally miserable, wondering how we had gotten into this state of matrimony. I wanted to be an actress, but for some reason I got it into my head that I wanted a baby. The pill was getting to be popular and Steven wanted me to take the pill. He wanted to study, but I wanted lace curtains if I couldn't be an actress.

"So that was the beginning of our most unholy of rows. I told Steven I was pregnant, testing the waters, so to speak. I was late, but I was sure I wasn't pregnant. And yet I wanted to be. I yelled at him that he should be a man, he wasn't a man, and so on and so forth, and he said he was leaving me. He'd put a shirt in a suitcase and I'd take it out. It was my suitcase, you see, the one my poor mother had bought me for my sixteenth birthday. The suitcase I planned to take to London to begin my acting career. The suitcase we used to elope with. And there was Steven planning to steal my suitcase!

"But he got the suitcase away from me, piled everything in, and started for the stairs. I barred his way, he pushed me, and that is how I broke my arm. So it was not entirely unprovoked.

"Now you want to know what happened next? Steven was so frightened he did go home to his mother, who hired a taxicab and took me to the hospital. I said I'd fallen down the stairs, which in fact I had.

"Our two mothers got together and decided we had better separate before we killed each other. I was let go at the fish-and-chip place as I couldn't carry orders. When my arm healed, I did head for London, where a friend and I decided to try Canada. The big acting career was a no-go, but in Montreal I had no trouble finding a position with the Bank of Montreal. It's not an acting career, but I've done well at the bank, taking courses at night. I started as a lowly teller, but I've been a manager since I transferred to Toronto. I had some vacation time coming to me over the holidays, or you would not have found me at home.

"And there you have it and I swear that I have not seen or heard from Steven since he has been in Canada."

"It's an incredible story."

"I really don't think your Allison has anything to worry about with Steven. Unless of course he's charged with trying to murder that poor woman. It really was an accident, more or less, when I went down the stairs."

"But he does have a temper." I bit my lip. "If Gracie demanded morphine and he wouldn't give it to her and she threatened to tell Allison about something he'd told Gracie, your arm for instance, he might have lost his temper again. She could have threatened to expose him as a wife-beater, which wouldn't have done his reputation as a physician any good."

"Steven would not have given that woman morphine unless she needed it for pain. He was one of the most honest people I have ever met. One time I found a wallet containing hundreds of pounds in the street and Steven insisted on turning it over to the police. I was all for having a good time with the money! Ironic, isn't it, that I became a banker? He should have become the banker, although he would have found it boring, I think.

"Let me show you a picture of us as the happily married pair. I don't know why I saved the thing, but there you are."

I recognized Sandra right away. Her bony face was obscured by lanky, stringy hair and her eyes were raccoon-like with heavy black eyeliner.

"We weren't even matched physically, were we?" she asked, pointing at the thick-chested young man with the heavy features and curly dark hair.

Who looked nothing like the Steven MacLeod I had met.

## Chapter Twelve

Back at Hendricks, I could hear voices— Jonathon's, presumably, and Jake murmuring soothing responses— coming from Jake's office. "And I said, 'No way am I guilty of what she's accusing me of,' but her goddamn brother says that she doesn't lie and to get out of his house." "Really, that's too bad, Jon." "If I could just talk to her. I suppose she's gone to one of those damn shelters or something." "Maybe if you just let her be for a while." "And have her spread those stories? No, I want her to tell me to my face and then we'll see who's telling the truth."

"So much for the sensitive poet," Molly sighed, sinking beside me on the couch. "Look at them, with their poses for the cameras, their sunglasses and funny hats." She indicated a pile of publishers' catalogues. I found it hard to concentrate, but I glanced at the picture of a young woman, last year's up-and-coming new poet with long frizzy hair hiding a tiny, still face. I'd met her somewhere— at a reading? A meeting? The still face was a pose, of course. Her act, her image. The opposite page showed a man in black leather, the black leather creating his persona...

None of them had anything on the man in the photo I'd photocopied from Sandra's honeymoon picture, I thought. I knew I had to go to the police. I was pretty sure now that Steven, or whoever he was, had tried to kill Gracie.

"Listen to that asshole," Molly said.

"I guess I'm just sour from living with my pampered poets for so many years," Molly said when I didn't reply.

I had to get out of there.

"I have to run, Molly. Can you please see that Jake reads that manuscript?"

"I told you I'd break his arm."

She didn't see me frown at the expression.

I phoned Neil, who sounded happy to hear from me. He'd be in Hamilton right away, he said, and he was there forty-five minutes later.

I was glad to see him.

"So that is that," I told Neil in the restaurant at the Holiday

Inn in Hamilton. The picture of the real Steven MacLeod lay between our club-sandwich specials on the table. "I think he did it all right."

"Or he could have found her and panicked," Neil said.

"Or Gracie could have found out the truth about him, told him and he hit her. Maybe she tried to blackmail him or something."

"Or something. Somehow Gracie and blackmailing don't seem to go together."

"Well, something happened. What I don't understand is how he could be in contact with the real Steven MacLeod's family and be able to fool them."

"He had to know the real Steven. He could have copied his handwriting. Typed the letters, even."

I had already spoken to Marion. Allison, predictably, was hysterical. But who wouldn't be in her place? First, her fiance is suspected of attempted murder and runs away, and then her beloved turns out to be someone else entirely.

"There have been cases of people mascarading as doctors, even performing surgery, and getting away with it for years. Like Steven, or whoever he is, they were generally well-liked by their patients."

"Steven wanted to be well-liked. He even made house-calls. He did deliver babies, but midwives and neighbours have done that. But he also did appendectomies and other simple operations. He'd promised Allison a trip to Scotland!"

"And then Gracie comes along and makes him realize his show can't go on forever. She went to his place Christmas Eve, didn't she? She strikes me as being one nosy person. She could have found something there. Poked through the medicine cabinet. Searched his desk while he was in the john. Whatever. Or she got him drinking and before he knew it, he was spilling his guts."

Neil looked at the picture of the real Steven MacLeod. He would be turning it over to the Ontario Provincial Police, who would contact Interpol.

"Poor Allison," I sighed, looking at the picture. The Steven MacLeod I had met appeared much nicer than the real one, who had a more determined look to him. I could well imagine the real Steven in a rage. Sandra might have provoked him, but I could imagine that strong face contorted in anger, the eyes bulging with fury. It was a look I recognized. My ex-husband had had that look, as did the poet Jonathon. You had to tiptoe warily around those men, and I was sure Sandra's Steven would have felt resentment to women in general after his first, disastrous marriage. And yet, Sandra said she had pushed him into marriage. Perhaps he had a strong Calvinist strand? Marriage had to follow sex? A dutiful son, a dutiful husband with a distinctly undutiful but strong woman?

If only there was a logical explanation for everything!

"Well, we'll soon find out who our Steven MacLeod really is. Maybe the real Steven's family will recognize the impostor. I feel there has to be a connection between the two men."

Neil tucked the photocopy into the briefcase he had brought with him and dipped a french fry into ketchup. "It gets more tangled and more tangled, doesn't it?"

"I'll say." I helped myself to one of his fries; mine were all gone. "Christmas wasn't so merry after all," I mused, raising my head to see Peter entering the restaurant. Neil's head swivelled to follow my gaze. Peter was wearing the toque his mother had given him for Christmas and he didn't look too happy, but he kissed me hello.

"They tried your room and I thought you'd be here."

"I had to give Neil the picture of the real Steven MacLeod," I explained. "He's taking it to the OPP."

"And onto Interpol and our friends at Scotland Yard," Neil said, making room for Peter to sit beside him.

"You must have driven right down as soon as I called Marion," I told Peter.

"I was coming anyway. I should have come with you in the first place to keep you company. Although I guess Neil was good enough to keep you company."

There was the slightest sarcastic and resentful edge to Peter's voice, but if Neil heard, he didn't let on.

"Here's the real Steven MacLeod," he said, producing the picture. Peter tried to feign disinterest, but he bent over the photocopy. He shook his head and said he wished Allison could have a copy. Neil said he'd make a copy at the hotel— they were sure to have a copier— and left to do so.

"Where's Conrad?"

"In the car. Where else? I borrowed Mom's car, by the way."

"I doubt if they allow dogs here in the hotel."

"I thought we'd go home."

"But I want to be close to the hospital."

"Guelph is only half an hour away. Come home at least for tonight. You can check on Gracie, and then we'll go home. You could be back here bright and early tomorrow. I think we could both use a peaceful night at home."

"Our home sweet home that was broken into."

"That's another reason to come back to Guelph. I can stay at the house and you can come back to the hotel tomorrow night if you have to. But let's have a night at home, okay?"

"If you had left Conrad up north you could have stayed here with me."

"Conrad on his own in Meredith? Dad's dying to get him into the woods. Conrad could get lost or caught in a trap. Get mistaken for a deer. You know guys hunt deer out of season up there."

Neil hung between us. We were both avoiding discussing him, I knew, and when Neil returned with another copy, Peter even asked him if he wanted another coffee.

"I'd better make tracks," Neil said. "Get the picture off. I could arrange to have a photo faxed to Meredith if you like."

"Why don't we send it to the lodge?" I suggested. "Marion and Hugh don't have a fax machine and I'm sure Allison wouldn't want it to go to the police station in Meredith."

Neil said: "The Meredith police will get a copy anyway. This is going to be big news."

Peter and I drove to the hospital in separate cars. There was no change in Gracie, and after a half-hour vigil at her bedside, we drove home to Lancaster Street.

Conrad was overjoyed to be home and settled with a big sigh on the sofa while Peter lit a fire. I turned the tree lights on and heated up some soup. We ate in front of the fire and finished the bottle of raspberry wine that my friend, Emma, had given us the week before Christmas.

We didn't mention Neil, and we were mellow when we went to bed at midnight. Soon Conrad was snoring peacefully at my feet. Gracie and the attendant problems seemed a million miles away as I snuggled into Peter's arms.

And dreamed of Neil. We were walking hand-in-hand through prairie grass, yellow wheat and blue flowers. Neil said, "I dreamed of this, too." And: "I'm just a prairie boy at heart," and suddenly we were in a country kitchen and I was having a bath in a tin tub in front of the stove. A brass bed stood in the corner... "Carolyn," Neil said softly as I stood up.

I awoke with a dry mouth and thought, *You've been married to Peter for so long. You're bored.*

As if he knew about my dream, Peter grasped me, hard. The clock radio read 4:28. I was wide awake and needed a drink of water, but Peter clutched me when I tried to move. At last I fell asleep again.

## Chapter Thirteen

The Reverend Robert Browning was waiting in the lounge when I returned to McMaster Hospital the next morning. Did the man always have to grin in that stupid way? I wondered as he got to his feet. The clerical collar made his round face rounder, more childlike.

"I left your manuscript with my publisher yesterday," I told him.

"Awfully good of you. I don't know how I can thank you." He pumped my hand and squeezed it. For a nerdy, wimpy guy he had a strong shake.

"I liked your book a lot," I told him. "I read it straight through that night and called my publisher right away."

The grin spread.

"Of course I don't know what Jake will think. Sometimes these things take a while."

"Just getting it to an editor is a major step," he said. "That's my understanding from the writers' books. Getting it read in the first place. No editor has ever wanted to read it. One wonders how any writer gets started!"

"Awfully good of you, splendid, splendid," he murmured as he walked beside me to the Intensive Care unit. "I wasn't going to wait for you, but as I had my rounds to make anyway, I thought you wouldn't mind if I stopped by, especially as I have your books along. You couldn't autograph them, could you?"

The man had all my mysteries with him. I signed them to "the other Robert Browning" which caused a squealing kind of appreciative chuckle. Who would have thought this silly little man would write about rollicking sex?

"Would you like me to say a prayer for your friend?" he asked when I was through.

"Why not?"

"You know what they say about prayer," he twinkled, winking at me because his sleuth frequently prayed his nympho wife would leave his zipper alone.

Gracie seemed a bit restless. Her lips twitched as "the other Robert Browning" prayed that God would heal her and bless her.

Reverend Browning didn't leave when he was through. After some consoling words about Gracie and questions about her family, he returned to the subject of writing and writers. Was it true, did I think, that once you had one book published, it was easier to get the next one out? It was all reputation, wasn't it? Doris Lessing had published a novel under another name and not done as well with it until the real author was revealed. And hadn't someone, a few years back, sent famous short stories to the CBC competition and had them rejected? Did I think William Faulkner would get published today?

"How do you think your novel will be received by your congregation?" I asked him.

He flexed his fingers.

"Oh, they'll say I am a bad boy, no doubt, but I'll cross that bridge when I come to it. The book won't seem quite real until it gets into print."

"Still, you have to consider that it could get published, sell a few thousand, make you a few dollars— and there you could be, out of a job. Everyone except your parishioners will have forgotten about the book. That's the reality of it."

"But if I had one published, surely another would follow? I have six written, actually."

"Six?"

"I used to put that in query letters until this fellow I know at the newspaper suggested I leave that fact out. Six failures, you see."

"You mean six books about the same sleuth?"

"All finished and ready to go. I write five pages a day, rain or shine," he said cheerfully. "My guy gets transferred in every second book, so the locale changes. Fun and games all the way. I think people like a laugh, don't you?"

I nodded and said that mysteries did quite well. Better than poetry, I said, wondering how Jake would feel about a whole raft of novels, all ready at once...

It should have been surreal sitting beside Gracie discussing the literary world, but it felt fine. I was grateful for Robert Browning's presence, actually, and found myself beginning to like this enthusiastic man.

Soon I was telling him about Steven MacLeod. Why not? It

would soon be in the papers, although I doubted if the revelation that the Meredith Steven MacLeod was an impostor would make the morning edition of the *Globe and Mail* or any other paper. Look out tomorrow, I thought. By then, the story would be wild in Meredith and it wouldn't take much for a reporter to track down some of Steven's patients.

I even told Browning about Gracie's apparent talent at discovering secrets, and soon I was revealing my boozy confession to her. It was surprisingly easy to talk to this benign little pastor. It was this benign quality that would make it easy for people to confide in him, I thought. Of course, the literary talk made for easy conversation between us. Put two writers together and they can talk all day about agents, publishers, markets and books.

But I did not tell him about my real attraction to Neil. Or the hug. Or the dream, which was troubling because it deepened the reality of the attraction, but was also private and sweet.

Gracie gasped.

"They say people in comas can hear," I said, lowering my voice. Gracie's lips moved. Was she coming to?

"Hearing is the last sense to go," Robert whispered.

We sat silently, staring at Gracie.

"I really know nothing about her," I said quietly. "A friend of mine suggested she might not even be my childhood friend, although that seems pretty far-fetched."

"Talking to her was like confessing to a priest, I think," Robert said. He was still whispering. "She should have learned about the secret of the confessional, though."

He glanced at his watch but made no move to leave.

"My ex-brother-in-law saw her, too, that day," I whispered. "The police have questioned him."

"Two suspects, then," Matthew said.

Gracie's lips moved.

"I do believe she can hear us," I said. "Gracie? Gracie?" I took her hand. "Squeeze my hand if you can hear."

Suddenly Gracie's face turned blue and the monitor on the machine went crazy. An alarm rang, and three nurses dashed into the room. Gracie's eyes flew open and stared blankly.

"Out! Please leave!" a nurse yelled as a young doctor ran into the room. Over my shoulder I saw the doctor bending over Gracie's chest.

Robert Browning's hand was on my elbow. The grin was gone from his face as he led me to the waiting area.

"They'll do everything they can, I'm sure," he said.

The room swam around me. Gracie was going to die. I knew it. She had been comatose for so long and it hadn't really seemed real that she could die. *Would die*, I thought, as my head swam.

"Put your head between your knees," Robert Browning said. "Do you want me to get a nurse?"

"She's going to die," I said, feeling his hand on my neck. An alarm went off. Footsteps, running.

And suddenly Neil was there. I burst into tears. His strong arm went around me as Robert Browning explained.

"Now that your husband's here, I'll see about that glass of water."

"Just a good friend," Neil explained, but Robert Browning was already going for the water.

I sat up.

"She had some kind of seizure. I think her heart stopped. Everyone came running. She's going to die. If you could have seen her eyes, Neil..."

"I had a feeling something was wrong," Neil said.

He sounded uncomfortable. Maybe he had had a dream, too?

"I have to be at work by two, and I thought I'd just nip over to see how things were."

I straightened up and wiped my eyes with my hands. "I need a tissue but I left my purse by Gracie's bed. They shooed us out."

Neil handed me a clean, ironed handkerchief.

"Christmas present," he explained. "Straight from the package."

"They should have let me stay."

"Sometimes these things aren't pretty. People get upset. Get in the way."

"But she has no one else, Neil."

"I know."

"I almost fainted. It was such a shock."

Robert Browning returned with the water. I made introductions.

"They're still working on her," he said.

"I have this awful feeling," I said. "I feel so guilty. I've been suspecting all kinds of things, but if she dies it's going to be awful."

"It wouldn't be your fault," Neil said.

"I invited her for Christmas. Unfortunately." I sipped the water. It was tepid. Neil took the cup from me. I leaned back and closed me eyes.

"Try and relax," Neil said. "Are you okay? Take deep breaths if you think you're going to faint."

"I'm okay. It just happened so fast. We were sitting there talking and she turned blue and then her eyes opened and she had the most terrible look."

"Talking about books," Robert Browning put in ruefully. "I'll just check, shall I?"

"I wish I didn't have to work this afternoon," Neil said when we were alone. "We've got two fellows off over the holidays or I'd call in sick."

"I'll be all right, Neil."

"It's the funniest thing, Carolyn. I woke up at seven and tried to get back to sleep because I'd planned on sleeping in, but all I could think of was that something would happen today. I almost didn't come to Hamilton, but then I thought, what the hell. Why not?"

"I'm glad you're here."

"Your colour's coming back. You were so white when I arrived."

"What if she dies? We wouldn't know how to contact her family. If there is a family."

"I'm hoping for some answers soon," Neil said. "Maybe I should have called Peter before driving to Hamilton."

"You didn't?"

"No. Should I have, do you think?"

"It's okay."

"It's no big deal anyway," said Neil as Robert Browning returned.

The man's grin was back. They had Gracie stabilized, he said, but her condition was critical.

"And I really must be off. I've a meeting with the church accountant at eleven-thirty."

Gracie's face was no longer blue, but there was a peaked sharpness in her features. Or did I imagine this? I wondered, sitting down by her bed. She seemed stiller, too.

"We were there in seconds," the nurse assured me. "Sometimes we have to work much longer to get the heart going again."

"Maybe you should call Peter," Neil said. "I have to leave soon, but you shouldn't be alone."

"I'll be okay. It was stupid, almost fainting like that."

"You couldn't help it," Neil said kindly, and then he was telling me about the first person he had ever used CPR on. The woman later accused him of stealing her brooch...

It was a funny story, and might have sounded crass coming from anyone else's lips, but Neil's humour was light and soon I was almost laughing.

If I could laugh, Gracie would not die.

Neil left at twelve-thirty. I walked him to the exit.

"Keep those doughnuts coming," I said.

Peter arrived at two o'clock with the news that Joe, of all people, had arrived in Guelph at ten o'clock!

"Why on earth would he do that? Running away from the police, the fool?"

Peter shrugged and looked at Gracie for a minute. There was more colour in her face and I doubted if he realized the seriousness of the morning's event. I had told Peter right away that Neil had dropped by, but he seemed more interested in the news about Joe.

"He's scared out of his wits. 'Scared shitless,' is how he put it. He seems to think he can find Steven, or whatever the bastard's real name is, by coming south. I think he plans to drive around Toronto in his truck. Someone in Meredith said that Steven had mentioned enjoying the marina at Harbourfront."

"In the middle of winter? That's just like Joe," I said. But I realized then, that after years of seeing Joe as Allison's redneck husband, which was the Hall family mythology, I felt some affection and understanding for him. His revelations to me had made him seem more like a real person. "Poor guy— as if Steven would walk around Toronto for anyone to find him. He'd be too smart for that. Joe must have panicked. The police don't really suspect him, do they?"

"Who knows? He keeps saying he's afraid they'll arrest him and put him away for the rest of his natural life. I told him not to leave the house. The guy's always had a few grey cells missing, if you ask me. Here you are, keeping a vigil by the bed of the woman he might be suspected of trying to kill, and there he is, in our house. He also wants to talk to the real Steven MacLeod's ex-wife."

"Well, there's no point in that. Our Steven had nothing to do with the real Steven's ex."

"And driving around Toronto!" Peter snorted.

"I suppose it would make Joe feel as if he was doing something."

"We keep calling that guy Steven," Peter said. "I wonder what his real name is. Allison still believes he's a doctor, by the way. She thinks it's all a mistake, that Steven MacLeod is a pretty common name."

"But she's talked to Steven's— the real Steven's family— and they told her about Sandra!"

"I almost believe, in the mood she's in now, that Allison thinks she'll stick with the guy whatever happens."

"Visions of visiting him in the pen, holding hands while the guards are watching," I said.

"I almost wish she'd go back with Joe," Peter said. "If it came to that."

"Why should she do either? She can live without a man in her life."

But I doubted this and Peter didn't answer. He suggested we go out for a bite to eat and I accepted.

It felt good to get out of the hospital and we went to a bistro on King Street in Westdale and had a late lunch of bean soup and quiche. We also picked up newspapers. Both the *Toronto Star* and the *Globe* had stories about Steven. The *Globe* was restrained, but the *Star* reporter had interviewed Meredith area residents who were "astonished and shocked." "Disbelieving." The man posing as Dr. Steven MacLeod was "caring, compassionate, competent." He had come out "in all kinds of weather." He had delivered a baby to a mother who had previously required Caesarians. He had stitched up wounds, set broken ankles and operated three times for appendicitis.

"Who is this man?" the cutline asked beneath a photo of Allison's "Steven MacLeod." The paper also showed the real Steven MacLeod and quoted his mother, during a telephone interview, as saying she was "distressed and puzzled." Her son had written her for Christmas and sent a parcel containing maple syrup, a colourful book about Canada and a pewter plate.

Allison was mentioned, but "Ms. Hall could not be reached for comment."

"I bet Allison packed the parcel. She must have bought the plate in the gift shop in Meredith," I said. "I think Neil was right. He said that our Steven and the real man had to know each other."

"How long was Neil here this morning? And why didn't you call me when all that happened?"

"Because it all happened so quickly! I almost fainted. Then Neil dropped in, but Gracie had just had the crisis and he stayed a while. And then it was over." Peter frowned. "Oh, stop it! What about Lorna? This is silly. I don't go on about the old flame you sneaked lunch with."

I wondered if Peter had dreams about Lorna. I wasn't lying to Peter. I thought I wouldn't want to know if he did dream about Lorna.

"Gracie did say you had an affair with Neil."

"You know that's not true. I didn't and that's all I am going to say."

"It's just that she said it," Peter said. "It wasn't the greatest thing to hear, believe me. I mean, okay, I know you didn't have an affair with Neil. But she did say it. When someone says something like that to you, it stays with you."

"Maybe she can't help it. Maybe she's mentally ill on top of everything else," I said. "I just wish I hadn't invited her, that's all." How often had I said this in the past few days? "Anyway," I went on, changing the subject, "now that the picture of the real Steven MacLeod has been published, someone is bound to come forward who recognizes him."

"Steven, the one we knew as Steven, even came to an interview in Meredith," Peter said. "He stayed with Mom and Dad and was back two weeks later to start work. The hospital had checked his references and everything seemed a-okay."

"How did he pull that off? The Meredith Steven would have known they'd check references."

"That's a good name for him. The Meredith Steven. Should we have some of that wonderful cheesecake?"

"I should really get back to the hospital. But let's live dangerously."

"We've been living dangerously ever since Gracie arrived," Peter said.

It was after three by the time we returned to the hospital. Peter stayed until four, and I remained until six. Gracie was holding her own.

Give Joe a case of Molson's beer and he's happy. We spent the evening going over and over everything: who was the Meredith Steven? Did I think Allison would stick with Steven? Did I think Allison was really in love with him?

We didn't think the police would really arrest Joe for what had happened to Gracie, did we? What if Joe went to prison for twenty-five years? Was that possible? It had happened, hadn't it, that honest people went to prison? Should he offer to take a lie-detector test? Should he inform the police where he was? Would they think he was guilty because he had left Meredith? We weren't aiding and abetting a criminal by letting him stay, were we?

Round and round the talk went, as the empties piled up. Finally Peter suggested Joe call the OPP. Tomorrow, Joe said; he'd call tomorrow. His mother knew where he was; it wasn't as if he'd fallen off the face of the earth.

"But maybe I should call," he said. "I don't know what to do. What about that friend of yours, the cop?"

"Neil, you mean. Why don't you call Neil? He's a pretty understanding guy."

Yes, no; yes, no. Joe dithered, and finally the problem was

solved for him because the doorbell rang, and it was Neil, with a big green scarf wrapped around his neck.

"Oh, Jesus," Joe said, taking his feet off the coffee table and standing up to shake hands as I introduced them. "Speak of the devil."

"And he's sure to appear," Neil finished. He asked me how Gracie was and made a point of mentioning that he had been at the hospital that morning. Peter seemed determined to show none of his earlier jealousy.

"Joe's been questioned about Gracie," Peter explained. "And now he's come 'down south,' as they say in the hinterland, to look for our phoney doctor."

"So you can tell your cop friends I haven't run away," Joe said. He was usually more reserved with strangers, but the beer had loosened his tongue. He offered Neil a beer and Neil accepted.

"But I hope you're not planning to go out looking tonight," he told Joe.

"Nah. I'm over the limit. Kind of crazy anyway, coming down here. Now that I think of it. He's probably in Mexico or Saudi Arabia by now."

"They're watching the borders," Neil said, "so unless he crossed the border the same night, which he could have done at the Soo, he won't get out of the country. Thanks, Peter. Nothing like a cold one on a cold night. So they questioned you, huh?" he asked Joe, although Neil already knew this.

Joe repeated the whole "sorry story," as he called it.

"And I wish I'd never laid eyes on that dame, that's all I can say."

"You and everyone else," I said.

"But it looks like I'm the only other suspect," Joe said. "That crazy dame. Not that I want her to die or nothing, but she sure caused a lot of trouble."

"That's why I'm here," Neil said.

"About Gracie? What did you find out? Not from your friend?"

"No, no. Just that Gracie checked out of a hotel apartment in downtown Chicago just before Christmas. That's all. No trace of her, no name for the next-of-kin. Her bank records gave the address of the hotel. She gave her occupation as private tutor. Paid the rent by cheque. She doesn't have a criminal record. She paid cash for her airplane ticket. She arrived a day before she said she did, but there's no record of where she stayed that night."

"Private tutor," I said.

"Tutor of what?" Joe asked.

"I wonder why she came a day early," I mused.

"Who knows? Making a delivery?" Neil speculated. "This is all off the record, by the way." He looked pointedly at Joe who raised a beer bottle in assent. "No one remembers her in the Soo. No Grace Forbes registered at a hotel."

"Maybe she used another name and paid cash. She had to stay somewhere that night," I said. "The Soo doesn't have that many hotels or motels. Maybe she has friends there."

"Or picked a guy up in a bar," Peter said.

"Yeah," Joe agreed.

"How long was she at this hotel place in Chicago?" I asked Neil.

"About a year. Claimed she was from New York."

"So now you've got people looking in New York," I said.

"Which is a pretty big place," Neil said. "You know what this sounds like, don't you?"

He looked at us.

"I bet she's a hooker, call girl," Neil said. "That would be my guess. Probably working for a pricey escort service, which could explain why she's never been caught. I'd say she was a teacher once, which explains the 'private tutor' bit. Most people aren't too inventive about themselves."

"Like she talked about her adoptive grandmother because she remembered my grandmother," I said. "And being a high-class hooker would explain why she was so entertaining. I guess some of those women don't just do sex. A man might want a dinner companion. A good dinner followed by bed."

Peter shook his head.

"Of course this is all conjecture," Neil said. "She could very well be some kind of private tutor."

"Yeah, like a sex tutor," Joe said, standing up to get another beer.

"I still have to check private schools in Chicago. Get to the library," I said. "I wish I had that library fax from North Bay."

"I forgot to tell you, Carmel's off sick," Peter said. "That's why it never came. She called the lodge. She was busy and forgot that day, and the next day she woke up with tonsillitis. Anyway, the police found out she claimed to be a private tutor."

"But Gracie told you the name of her school wasn't flowery like the Lily Becker School, which she found out about by going through my purse, the sneak!"

"There is no record of Grace Forbes teaching in any school in Chicago, private or public," Neil said.

"I can't believe how gullible I was," I said. "Didn't Gracie leave a forwarding address or something at the hotel?"

"She said she was moving to Canada, that she'd found a

full-time teaching position. She asked them to hold her mail until she got a permanent address."

"What mail?"

But Neil didn't have this information.

"Probably nothing significant or it would have been mentioned."

"Not even Christmas cards?" I asked.

"Probably not. And if there had been any, the police would have contacted the people sending them. She might have had another address in the city somewhere. But you wrote to the hotel address, and the telephone number you had matched her phone."

"I just don't understand any of it," I mused as Joe returned with four opened beer bottles. He passed us each one. "If Grace Forbes did not register at a hotel in the Soo, she could have used another name. Maybe she taught under another name, too. But why all the subterfuge?"

"She certainly did not expect trouble," Peter said. "She didn't come to Meredith expecting to be almost killed."

Neil disagreed. He thought someone like Gracie would be extra cautious.

"And my bet is— again, I'm just guessing— that she came early just to look the place over. Test the waters, see what it felt like. She didn't rent a car, though, and apparently only took a taxi the once. I shouldn't really have this second beer."

"Ah, go ahead," Joe said. "Who's gonna arrest a cop?"


After Neil left ("Doughnuts next time," he whispered to me as I saw him to the door) and Peter went to bed, Joe became philosophical. What was the point of life, of love, of kids and marriage, if it all ended in unhappiness? Who knew what tomorrow would bring? You went along and did your best and worked to support your wife and kids and one day the "the rug was pulled from beneath your feet?"

By this time Joe was on what had to be his eighth beer. If he was maudlin, he was also truly perplexed. I'd had more real conversations with Joe in the past week than in the entire time I'd known him previously. Peter and I had always dismissed him as a redneck, and both Marion and Hugh hadn't liked him as Allison's husband. But the divorce had made Joe examine his life and he had become a much more interesting person, I thought.

"She was always saying she was unhappy," he said of Allison, "but it never hit home. Wives gripe, you know? Ma was always nagging and griping when Pa was alive. That's just the way it was. Do you think if I'd let her take nursing it would have made a difference, Carolyn?"

"Think of what you said. Let her? What does that mean? Why should you let her do anything? She's her own person."

"Yeah, you're right." He sighed, picked up the beer bottle, took a swig and made a face. He'd had enough, he said, flicking the button on the remote control. A TV evangelist was selling a leather-bound Bible. You could order a rhinestone ring with a FREE matching bracelet for $29.95. Tavern doors swung open in a western.

And then Gracie's rich voice filled the room.

## Chapter Fourteen

"Are you worried?" Gracie asked. "Are you lonely or homesick? Do you feel the whole world is against you and that no one understands? Why not give Mother a call and tell her all about it? Mother can help. Mother will understand. Mother will listen. Mother will give you advice."

A 900 number flashed across the screen, followed by the statement that all major credit cards were accepted.

Luckily, the crossword puzzle Peter had been working on and a pen lay on the coffee table and I was able to scribble down the number while a weepy middle-aged woman attested to the power of Mother Love.

"Just when I thought there was nothing to live for, Mother helped me. I had lost my job, my husband had deserted me and my teenaged daughter had run away from home. I had nowhere to turn, but Mother helped me to see the light at the end of the tunnel. Mother..."

But I was already dialling the 900 number. I had to borrow Joe's credit card because my purse was in the kitchen.

"Welcome to Mother who's *so* glad you called! She has been waiting for your call and will be right with you as soon as you give me your credit card number."

Another voice, not Gracie's, but still warm and sympathetic, came on the line after I gave Joe's Visa number.

"Hello, hon. I've been sitting by the phone hoping you'd call tonight. How're you doing, sweetheart?"

"Not so great, actually."

"Ah, honey, that's too bad. What's happening?" the voice

purred. It was low and husky, a typical chainsmoker's voice, I thought. "I've been so worried."

"My best friend is in the hospital. Someone tried to kill her and they don't know if she'll live or die," I said.

"Oh, baby. How awful for you. She's your very best friend? How long have you known her?"

"Since I was a girl. She came to stay with my grandmother and me. I'm calling from Canada, by the way, from a little place near Toronto. My friend's name is Grace, but I always called her Gracie."

Silence.

"She came to spend Christmas with me. She's been in a coma since Boxing Day. We're trying to reach her family, but we haven't had any luck. And then I heard her voice coming from the television. My name is Carolyn Archer. Maybe Gracie mentioned me to you."

I heard whispers, followed by coughing.

Another voice spoke. This one was brisker, with a slight New Jersey accent. The supervisor? I wondered. I knew some of the Canadian "helplines" originated from a plaza outside of Toronto, where single mothers and older women who couldn't get other jobs manned the telephones in a single room. I could picture a room of bored and overweight women sitting in cubicles in Chicago.

"How can I help you?"

"This is about Grace Forbes. Gracie. My name is Carolyn Archer and Gracie's in a coma after someone tried to kill her."

If this woman was a friend, I hadn't been very tactful. But the call was costing me— Joe— $3.00 a minute.

"I recognized her voice on TV," I said. "Isn't there another number I can call? I don't like spending $3.00 a minute to talk."

"Forbes isn't Grace's last name."

"Then she's using another name. She's tall, with reddish hair. She uses a lot of make-up and is well-dressed. Maybe she told you she was visiting her sister in Canada."

"Give me your number and I'll call you right back," the voice said.

The phone rang immediately.

"All right, I'm in a private office now and we can talk. There's no need for everyone to hear this. You are Carolyn Archer?"

"One and the same. The mystery novelist."

"Grace's sister."

"Actually not. Not really. We called each other sisters for a while when we were kids."

"She said she was going to visit her sister in Canada. I drove her to the airport myself. I'm her vice-president of operations and acting president while Grace is away. What's this about Grace in the hospital?"

"She's been unconscious since Boxing Day," I began. I decided not to mention the morphine business, and I played down Gracie's manipulations, merely saying that I thought Gracie might have heard something which put her life in danger, but I reported the rest, even telling this woman— Sonia Chosnick, as she introduced herself— about Steven and his mysterious disappearance.

I was aware that I sounded inappropriately elated. It all fit together beautifully. Why hadn't I thought that Gracie would be in such a business? No wonder she could get secrets out of people! She was used to hearing the deepest and darkest secrets night after night from lonely people who watched late-night television and didn't mind paying for someone to listen.

And she wasn't a prostitute after all, I thought, as Joe handed me another beer. I heard the toilet flushing. Peter must have gotten up, I thought, as Sonia talked about the Mother Line and Grace. Not Gracie, but Grace. Grace took everything to heart and people were always trying to meet her. Maybe someone had found out she was going to Canada and followed her there?

Maybe the mysterious doctor had called the Mother Line and Gracie recognized his voice?

But I couldn't imagine Steven, whoever he was, doing this.

"You don't know all the kooks out there in the world," Sonia said. "Sometimes they think they're space aliens and only last week this guy said he was Jesus. Like, you never know. But we are careful to protect all our Mothers. We fire them if they connect privately with any of the callers. That goes for all the lines. We don't just have the Mother Line, but Mother's the only one you get up there. I guess I'm in a state of shock about Grace. It hasn't hit me yet."

"You don't know where we can reach her family?"

"What's going on?" Peter asked from the doorway. I motioned for him to keep quiet. And to keep Conrad, who had followed him down the hall, from barking.

"I understood you were her only relative," Sonia said. "Her parents died in a tragic car accident years ago. I wouldn't know who to tell you to call."

So Gracie hadn't been adopted after all. If she had been adopted and the parents died, she would have played that tragedy up.

"Gracie spoke about a grandmother."

"The old lady in Maine. Yeah. But she's long gone. Maybe I should come up to Canada. But I got three new girls working here and I don't know if Grace would want me to leave. It's a big responsibility. You call her Gracie?"

"I always have."

"She is going to be all right, isn't she?"

"It's too early to tell."

"Gee. I had a feeling something would happen. I told Grace it would be cold up there and the wolves and everything... Maybe I should fly up."

"I think the police will be in touch."

Sonia wasn't too pleased to hear this, even though everything at Mother's was "above board, strictly legal."

Before hanging up, Sonia gave me the office number at Mother Line. I would call her in the morning, I said, to report on Gracie's condition.

"What the hell is going on?" Peter asked.

Joe had pressed mute on the remote control. I turned the sound up and once again Gracie's voice filled the room while a plump, motherly woman rocked on a verandah.

"There is no one who understands like Mother," Gracie said as the screen showed a bus stopping at a farm gate. "Travel the world—" the scene now was the Eiffel Tower— "but you will never find another heart that hurts when you hurt, laughs when you laugh and rejoices when you rejoice." The motherly woman embraced an earnest young man as he dropped his suitcase beside a farm gate. Switch to a younger mother in sepia, gazing adoringly at her infant.

"Mother loves you," Gracie said.

I switched the TV off.

"You didn't call the Mother Line one lonely night, did you, Joe? Maybe that's how Gracie knew just what to say to you."

Joe looked completely sober now.

"Are you kidding? I've got enough with Ma."

Peter turned the set back on. A thin man with a huge Adam's

apple was weeping. He'd been estranged from his mother for ten years...

"But Johnny came home," Gracie said.

"What a scam," Peter said with delight.

## Chapter Fifteen

I spent the next day with Gracie. She was restless; her limbs twitched and she opened her eyes several times, although without, I thought, recognizing me. Her eyes looked perplexed, as if she knew she was in a strange place. A doctor stopped in for a few minutes and said he thought Gracie was showing signs of coming around.

I had called Sonia at nine, before leaving for the hospital, and learned that the police had already been in touch.

"But we still don't know very much, do we, Gracie?" I said. "You seem to have had two lives, one at the hotel under the name Forbes and an entirely different life at Mother Line.

"Mother Line," I repeated, bending over her, but there was no reaction. "Not adopted, were you? So Reg is the only one you have. If he's still alive...

"But I have to admit I admire you for getting away with so much BS. You tell a good story. You've invented yourself over and over, haven't you? If only you hadn't gone too far, everything would have been fine. You could have gone back to Chicago as the private school teacher and we would never have known who you really were.

"But we still don't know, do we, Gracie?"

I continued talking to her most of the day, saying the same things over and over, thinking to myself that Gracie and Steven— the Meredith Steven— were a lot alike. I thought, too, of Anna Anderson, turning herself from a simple Polish farmgirl into the Grand Duchess Anastasia. People wanted to believe, I thought. You were who you presented to the world. As a cookbook author, Carolyn Archer was nice and cosy. As the writer of pioneer mysteries, Carolyn Archer became A Canadian Writer. As the author of a popular mystery publicized and selling in the States, Carolyn Archer had become A Celebrity.

It was all image, I thought, remembering the catalogues at Hendricks, with the posed poets in the frizzy hair or shorn heads.

Peter and Neil joined me at three. I had called Neil the night before with the news about Mother Line and he had passed the information on to the OPP in Meredith.

It was Neil's day off and he had gone to see Peter at The Bookworm. They had both resolved, I thought, to be buddies.

Their main news was that Allison, unable to sit still in Meredith, had joined Joe in Guelph. She and Joe were going to Toronto to speak to Sandra MacLeod and to show Steven's (the Meredith Steven's— I had to keep remembering this) picture to bartenders in bars and bistros along Harbourfront in Toronto.

"It won't do any good," Neil said in the cafeteria. They wanted to leave, but I was determined to remain in the hospital in case Gracie regained consciousness. "Steven could be anywhere by now, but someone may recognize him."

"No word on the real Steven MacLeod?"

"He worked in a walk-in clinic in North York before leaving for Meredith," Peter said. He glanced at Neil. The revelation about

Gracie's true identity had made Peter happier. She was obviously a liar and therefore had lied about my "affair" with Neil.

"So the two men changed identities between Toronto and Meredith. But before the interview. So something happened to the real doctor. Did the real Steven's family recognize our Steven?"

"They have no idea who he is," Neil said. "All they know is that their Steven had made some Scottish friends in Toronto."

"The real Steven MacLeod applied to work in Meredith, then," I said, "but our Steven turned up for the interview and got hired. Does that mean the real Steven is dead? He has to be, or the Meredith Steven wouldn't have taken the chance he did. The real Steven must have lived somewhere in Toronto."

"A sub-let," Neil said. "He moved just before the Meredith interview. And he quit the clinic before the interview, after an altercation with another doctor. The real Steven wasn't as mild as Allison's Steven."

"He did break his wife's arm," I said. "But why hasn't anyone come forward who knew the Meredith Steven?"

"Maybe he had a job like Gracie's," Peter quipped, "and no one ever saw his face."

Gracie did not regain consciousness that day and Allison and Joe were back in Guelph by ten without having had any luck. Joe had insisted on parking at a mall outside of Toronto and taking buses, which was the first problem: they got on the wrong bus. By six o'clock they had visited only three bars and no one recognized the man in Allison's picture. A bemused Sandra MacLeod fed them and Joe fixed her leaking kitchen faucet before returning by subway and bus to the mall where the truck was parked.

We all stayed up to watch Mother Line. Joe slept on the couch, and Allison in the spare bedroom.

# Chapter Sixteen

"So what about New Year's Eve?" Peter asked in the morning. Joe and Allison were still asleep and he had just come back from walking Conrad. "What are we going to do about that?"

"I guess it all depends on Gracie."

"I have to get Mom's car back to her anyway, but I was hoping you'd come too. Just for the night. We could drive up together in Mom's car and you could fly back down the next day."

"It would seem heartless to leave Gracie."

"Neil can sit with her. Christmas was a wash-out. If I didn't have to return the car we could have had a terrific New Year's Eve on our own, but Joe and Allison might still be here."

"Think about it," Peter said, raising my hand and kissing it. Was it my imagination, or was he more ardent since Gracie's talk about me and Neil? "It's only two days away. Gracie has spoiled enough."

I leaned against him. He was right. *Gracie was a liar.* There had been no affair with Neil. Dreams were not reality.

I said I'd drive to Meredith with Peter the day of New Year's Eve and fly back the next day unless something changed with Gracie.

But by December 31, not much had changed. Gracie was opening her eyes more and she continued with the twitching, but she had not regained consciousness. At ten o'clock in the morning Peter and I left for Meredith in Marion's bug.

Allison and Joe decided to stay in Guelph. They had spent another day in Toronto, and a bartender at a bar in a hotel near the waterfront thought he recognized Steven, and said the man worked in a bank on Bay Street. They found the man in question, who did look a little like Steven, although younger, working as a loan officer. They also visited the walk-in clinic where the real Dr. Steven MacLeod had worked, but no one there recognized the photo of Allison's Steven.

The police had been to the clinic before Allison, and Allison was alternately weepy and angry. She loved Steven; she thought it was a ghastly mistake. Steven was a criminal and should be locked up; she never wanted to see him again.

She snapped at Joe constantly. She had insisted on not parking by the mall the second day ("Don't be such a country hick!") and Joe grumbled about paying for parking in downtown Toronto. "Cheap, cheap, you've always been cheap!" Also, he kept getting lost in the big city.

Neil would be staying with Gracie.

"Isn't it a relief to get away?" Peter asked me, taking my hand. "Let's just enjoy New Year's Eve."

The problem with Allison and Joe remaining in Guelph was what to do with their kids on New Year's Eve while the adults went to the lodge. Marion could have sent the boys to Gladdie, but Gladdie would drink herself into a stupor as she watched the New Year's Eve festivities on TV.

"If only Hilary weren't helping out at the lodge, we could get her to stay," Marion said.

"Why do you need anyone?" Matthew asked. "I can look after the kids, get them to bed on time."

"Get them to bed! You know your mother promised you could all stay up until midnight," Marion said. "We don't want any rows."

"There won't be any 'rows.'" Matthew rolled his eyes at the English expression. "We don't need a sitter!"

"I don't want any calls at eleven that there's a row."

"There won't be. Honest."

"And don't touch the thermostat. Or make a fire. If there's any trouble..."

"... call 911," Matthew finished for her and made a face at me.

Peter was right: it was good to get away from Guelph. And from Gracie, too, I thought as we arrived at the lit-up lodge. It felt great to be wearing the new red caftan-type dress I'd bought for New Year's Eve weeks ago, and to have Peter in a good mood beside me.

Tiny fairy lights lit up the main salon at the lodge and red tapered candles lent a mellow glow. The Christmas tree was still standing, and small tables had been draped with green linen. Some of the Meredith hoi-polloi were present— Dr. Walker and his heavyset wife waved at me from across the room— and about twenty people who had come north for cross-country skiing from southern Ontario and New York and Michigan. A huge log burned in the fireplace and a place had been cleared for dancing. Linda had even hired a string quartet and a folk singer from North Bay.

We would dine the night away and drink champagne.

"This is all so wrong," Marion whispered as Hilary set down an oval platter of lox canapes. "I can't help but think that Allison and Steven should be here, as they'd planned," she said after Hilary was gone. "Instead, Steven has turned out to be an impostor and Allison's drinking beer with Joe in Guelph."

"Let's just enjoy ourselves," Peter told his mother. "It's out of your hands. Allison will do what she'll do."

"That's just what I'm afraid of," Marion sighed. She looked wonderful in a plum cotton dress with a bright green belt. And splendid, dangling papier-mache earrings.

"Be happy," Peter said, pouring champagne.

Marion hadn't mentioned Gracie, I thought.


But we were happy. Or became happy as we sipped champagne and dined leisurely on pepper bouillon, trout-in-aspic, racked lamb, dilled vegetables, salad and pate, and sherbet ice. Each course was accompanied by the appropriate wine, and there would be a sandwich buffet after midnight.

The folk singer sang "The Village Blacksmith" and "Joe Hill." The string quartet played schmaltzy fifties and sixties tunes as well as waltzes and Peter and I danced cheek-to-cheek to "Crying in the Chapel" and "Love Me Tender." I waltzed to "Tales of the Vienna Woods" with Hugh and the brassy couple, the Nickels, whom we'd met earlier in the week, insisted on sending a bottle of wine to our table because they had discovered, in the meantime, that I was A Famous Author.

"I hope you never never leave me," Peter whispered in my ear as we danced to another Elvis melody.

"Why should I leave you?"

Peter didn't answer, but pressed me against him.

"Love me?"

"Love you!"

I pushed Neil out of my mind.


It was quarter to twelve and Peter and I were holding hands when "the other Robert Browning" burst into the lodge.

"Is there any more room in the inn?"

His round face beamed above a red turtleneck as he handed his coat to Hilary. Behind him was a tall elderly woman in a mink coat. I quickly explained who he was to Linda and went over to him. He seized my hands and kissed me on both cheeks.

"You wonderful person, you! Your publisher wants to publish my novel! He phoned me and said you were here. Mother and I drove straight up!"

Mother frowned. No, she would not relinquish her mink.

"Announcement! Announcement!" the little pastor called out. He giggled. "You see before you, not a rude interloper, but an up-and-coming real live whodunit author!"

There was a startled silence, followed by, after a minute, applause. Linda sent Hilary to fetch two chairs, which she squeezed in at our table.

Mother surveyed the room with slitted eyes.

"I told you you should have worn a tie!" she hissed at her son.

The "up-and-coming author" had had only one glass of champagne by the time we began the countdown to the New Year (Mother ordered a "highball" from Hilary), but he seemed as high as the rest of us by the time the New Year came in with a tooting and rattling of the hokey tin toys the lodge had provided.

"Happy New Year!"

"Happy New Year!"

Peter gave me a big kiss on the lips and Hugh did the same, saying I was the best daughter-in-law in the world as we got up to sing "Auld Lang Syne." Robert Browning gripped my hand tightly in his. He hugged me when the song was finished.

Mother, however, guarded her mink and complained that she had not had her drink served yet. No, champagne would give her indigestion, she said; she wanted her highball and what kind of establishment was this anyway, or did they just cater to the rich and famous?

I giggled and she glared at me. I tried to catch Hilary's eye, but she was carrying glasses to the kitchen.

There were two other women washing up and placing dishes into the dishwasher. Dishes and glasses were everywhere and Hilary had to shove a pile of *New York Times Book Reviews* off the table where Linda usually sat to have her tea.

"Did you forget the old bat's highball?" I asked her. I began giggling again. "Should I order it from the bar? Or should I tell her to drink cake? I mean eat cake?"

"I'll get it." Hilary looked cross. And tired. There was always a little party for the staff after a lodge do, and I was just telling Hilary I wanted to buy her a drink when the kitchen telephone rang.

Matthew. Hilary handed the phone to me.

"Happy New Year, kid!" I babbled into the receiver.

But Matthew wasn't calling to wish me Happy New Year. He was calling to say that he had called his own phone in North Bay, to leave a New Year's message on the machine for when they returned home ("the kids wanted to do it") and Steven had answered.

"What did he say?"

"Nothing. He hung up right away but I could tell it was his voice. Should I dial 911 and tell the police?"

"No, I'll do it."

Peter was drinking champagne and listening to Mother and Robert Browning was dancing with Marion when I returned to our table.

"I told him it would be too cold for me with my lungs and my arthritis, but he insisted on coming up here," Mother said.

Peter hiccupped.

"Maybe you can talk to him. And that red turtleneck."

"Have a drink," Peter told her, hiccupping again. He winked at me.

"I would, but it seems they only care about the rich and famous here."

"I have to talk to you," I told Peter.

I didn't want to call the police. Not yet. Half of me was hoping that Steven would escape before the police got there. And the other half wanted to hear his story.

Peter was convinced that Matthew had just got a wrong number. "Why would Steven answer their phone? Forget it," he said, swaying as he stood up to head for the buffet.

Across the room the rising whodunit author grinned at me over a loaded plate of cold cuts and cheese. He threw me a kiss as I walked over.

"Want to go for a drive?" I asked him.

I didn't want to lie to Peter, and what I said wasn't a total lie, because as the pastor's big, comfortable dark Oldsmobile headed to North Bay, Robert Browning could talk only about his novel. He was to go to Jake's office to sign a contract on January 2! And Jake wanted to see the other manuscripts! Should he have sent them by courier? But January 2 was only one day away!

Allison's townhouse was dark when we arrived. Had Steven been in there, asleep, when the telephone rang, and picked it up out of habit?

Or had he been hoping that Allison, thinking he might be at her place, would call?

Had he answered because he wanted to be caught? I wondered, pressing on the doorbell.

There was no answer, but I sensed someone in there, listening. The townhouse on the other side was empty, I remembered; Allison had said the young teachers who lived there had gone to Florida for the Christmas break.

I kept the pressure on the bell. The pastor was looking uncomfortable now, without his habitual smile.

"I know Allison keeps a spare key in the garage. She told us where it was when we came to North Bay in the summer, but we didn't have to use it because she was home."

But the garage door was locked. I pressed the bell again and called out Steven's name.

I tried the door. It was open.

"You didn't have to do all that ringing after all, did you?" the pastor said nervously.

But if he had none of the bravado of his fictional sleuth, I had even less. What if Steven had committed suicide?

"Hello, Carolyn," Steven's voice said out of the darkness. He switched the light on.

He was sitting in the black leather swivel chair Allison had bought at Ikea. He needed a shave and he looked thinner, but he was— Steven. The same Steven. He gave me a weak smile.

"I thought someone would have found me before this." He had his hands folded in his lap and I noticed he was wearing Matthew's slippers.

"I think everyone thought you'd run away to Mexico."

I removed my boots at the door, and slung my coat over the railing dividing the vestibule from the living room.

"You've brought the police, then, have you?"

"No." I made introductions. "Everyone else was pretty drunk. We were at the lodge for New Year's Eve. Matthew called and said you'd answered the phone."

"Should not have done so. I was hoping Allison would come home, I suppose. It is New Year's Eve and I cannot even offer you a drink. Allison had a bit of beer and wine, but that's long gone. I could use a drink, actually."

"I'd help you if I could. But I didn't bring anything with me."

"Where is Allison?"

"She's in Guelph. She and Joe are trying to find a trace of you in Toronto."

"Joe, too?"

"He came down first. He saw Gracie that afternoon and wanted to do something. He's afraid he'll be arrested for her attempted murder. You know, don't you? It's been on the news?"

"Yes, I know. They're looking for me, but I had nothing to do with that."

"But you did go there that afternoon."

"Yes. Shall I make a pot of tea?"

I followed him to the kitchen, afraid he would run out the back door or hurt himself. He busied himself setting out mugs, measuring the loose tea which Allison had bought for him.

"Where is your car?"

"In Allison's garage. Where else?"

"You could have been in Mexico by now."

He nodded and gave a thin smile. "Better not to run," he said.

"But you did run."

"Not too far, surely?" He raised an eyebrow. "And I ran, if that is what you call it, before I knew about what had been done to your friend."

"You ran because of Gracie, though, didn't you?"

He filled the teapot, set it to steep, and poured milk into a pitcher I recognized as belonging to Marion's old set of china.

He sniffed the milk and said it was still fresh. But he was running out of things.

"So what were you planning to do?"

"Wait for Allison to come home," he said. "Explain everything to her. It wasn't logical thinking, I know. But I came here, let myself in with my key, and stayed. I should not have answered the telephone tonight, but I thought it might be Allison."

"And you were half asleep?"

"No, I was awake. I was planning to give myself up. It seemed the honest thing to do. I will have to now, won't I? But I was hoping to explain everything to Allison first. Shall we have our tea in the front room?"

"Let's just sit in the kitchen. I'll tell my friend."

But the pastor had fallen asleep, probably exhausted from adrenaline and excitement and the long drive north. And the bit of champagne.

"So."

"So."

Steven and I drank our tea.

"I don't know what to say," I said.

"What is there to say? It is true, I am not a physician."

"What is your real name, for a start?"

"That's the irony of it. My name *is* Steven MacLeod."

"You knew the doctor?"

"Just. We met at Banff in the summer. He had gone hiking and I was living nearby, in a cabin. To try the Canadian wilderness, you see. My old mother had died and left me the bit she had. There was not a great deal, but I had spent years looking after her, and I decided to strike out for Canada. There was a derelict cabin and I made it snug. I grew a beard, like a real pioneer, which is why no one recognized me. I suppose my picture has been in the newspapers? I saw it on television."

"Yes, you've made the papers."

"It's rather cliché-ish about the beard, but I kept to myself pretty much. Valuing the silence. I had enough money for two years, if I lived simply, and then I was going to go to Vancouver to work."

"As a doctor, I suppose."

"As a nurse. I'm a male nurse." He made a face. "Not a masculine occupation, some say. I wanted to become a doctor, but then Mother grew ill and that did make things difficult. She was not an easy woman. Her heart, you see, and she wouldn't hear of me moving away."

"And then she died."

"Yes. I thought she would live to be a hundred, but then, mercifully, she went to her heavenly reward, as she would have put it."

"And you came to Canada."

"I sold the house and came over, yes."

"And met Dr. Steven MacLeod."

"You will think it terrible, but I do not regret having done so. Taking his place showed me I could be a doctor."

"And for a while you were a doctor."

"Yes. And I met Allison, and has that not turned into a tragedy?"

"What about the real doctor?"

"He got lost. Oh, he was a difficult one. Wouldn't stay on the path. I think he would have died in the wilderness if I hadn't come upon him and brought him back to the cabin. He had quit his position at the clinic in anger and was to go for an interview in Meredith in two weeks' time. He could be his own boss there, you see. Have things his way. He had put his furniture in storage and was going straight to Meredith after his holiday."

"It must have seemed a coincidence, the two of you sharing a name."

"It was that. Divine providence, as my old mother would say. And then he died. Yes. He had a heart attack in the night and was gone in the morning. He was overweight, and had over-exerted himself, I suspect. He'd complained about indigestion, gas pains. And he died."

"What did you do with him?"

"I left him. The cabin was remote, as I have said, and at first I planned to hike out. Then I thought I had better take his wallet and things, in case someone broke in. He had the key to the storage unit in his pocket, and the airline ticket in his haversack... He had talked a fair bit about his family, and I found letters, photos."

"When you got to Toronto. With his ID and papers," I said.

"I had some idea at first of contacting his family, but by then I had abandoned his corpse and how could I explain that? I never planned on carrying out any deception, you see. I spent two days in Vancouver, just thinking things over. Nor did I use his airplane ticket. I took the train east, thinking all the way. Or not thinking.

"He was so terrible, you see. Not a nice or a kind person, and I got to thinking how unfair it was that this crude man should be a doctor. He bragged about women who were in love with him, patients who were throwing themselves at him."

"Did he tell you he'd been married? That his ex-wife was in Toronto?"

Steven shook his head.

"He said he had met a rich widow who wanted to marry him."

The pastor stirred in the living room.

"And so you came to Meredith. And met Allison."

"And met Allison, which is what I'm sorry for. Not for meeting her, but for deceiving her."

"Not for the rest?"

"I'm sorry I got into the situation, but I did no harm. Some good, I think. I'd assisted at operations, you see, and felt quite competent operating for appendicitis, for instance. I suppose you want to call the police now."

"I think you should call them yourself."

He nodded. "I really did not do anything to your friend."

"But she found out about you?"

"She had the real doctor's driver's license when I called on her, that day at your mother-in-law's. She said she wasn't feeling well and I went over."

"She asked you for morphine, didn't she?"

He nodded.

"And when you wouldn't oblige her, she showed you the driver's license?"

"She insisted on making us a snack. She must have gone through my desk while I was in the lavatory. I should have burned the license, but I somehow couldn't bring myself to throw it out."

"You wrote letters to the doctor's family."

"Typed them. As he did. There was a half-finished letter in his little machine, you see. Bragging sort of letters they were."

"But you were going to take Allison to Scotland."

"That was her idea. I was going to think of something."

"What happened to the driver's license?"

"I took it. She didn't try to stop me. She offered it to me, actually. But she knew, you see."

"And then you drove here?"

"Yes. And now I suppose I must turn myself in. I really did not harm your friend, Carolyn."

I nodded.

"Why don't you call Allison first?" I heard myself saying.

## Chapter Seventeen

If Peter hadn't had so much to drink he would have been furious at me, but I don't think he realized how long I'd been gone when I returned with Robert Browning. Most of the guests had gone to bed, but Peter, Marion and Hugh had joined Linda and Eric and the staff in the smaller lounge. The musicians had returned to North Bay and Hugh, very red in the face, was tinkling the piano keys.

Robert Browning's mother, I was amused to see, had had quite a bit to drink, but she still had her mink coat lying over the back of a chair.

The two older women were drinking beer and Hilary was sipping wine.

Peter pulled me down beside him onto the couch. "Got all the literary talk out of the way?"

"All the literary talk and a lot more."

But Peter wasn't interested. He was talking to one of the older helpers about her son, with whom he'd gone to school. Marion and Linda were tete-a-tete and Mother Mink grabbed her son.

I went into the kitchen and dialled my phone in Guelph. The line was busy. I felt completely sober again, and poured myself a glass of wine from the bottle on the counter, but as I tasted it, my stomach turned and I decided to make myself a cup of instant coffee.

Have a coffee and return to the lounge with the news about Steven, I thought. As I waited for the kettle to boil, I ducked into the powder room.

When I came out, Hilary was sitting at the kitchen table, smoking a cigarette and leafing through the *New York Times Book Review*. She looked startled, shoved the paper aside, and got up to pour herself more wine.

"I didn't know you smoked."

"You have to sneak cigarettes when you can these days."

"You must be exhausted, all this work."

"It's over, anyway." She shrugged and smiled at me. "It's work."

Her face was flushed. She didn't look as drab as she usually did. She was actually wearing a bit of make-up and her cheeks were red.

"I noticed you were reading *The New York Times Book Review*. I can save them for you, if you like."

"Sure." She took a drink of wine and looked at me. "It's something to read, anyway."

"You're a regular bookworm, aren't you? Did you get the Danielle Steele from the library yet?"

"Still waiting."

"But you don't really read Danielle Steele, do you, Hilary?" She started to speak, but I cut her off. "I think you take Danielle Steele books out of the library so no one will know anything about you."

"You're wrong." Her voice was level.

"Or maybe you read romance books because you want to write one. Make some money? But you can't, can you? Because you're not that kind of a writer, are you? You're a serious writer, isn't that right?"

I didn't look at her as I went on.

"I think you've published a book." She didn't respond. "A book of poetry, I'd say, and some pieces here and there in the literary magazines. Yet here you are: poor Hilary, dishwasher and cleaning lady. Marion said you came from Orillia, to get away from your abusive husband."

"I did come here to hide from my husband," Hilary said. "He broke my leg."

"Jealous, was he?"

Hilary didn't answer.

"But not jealous of other men, I suspect. Jealous of your recognition, the pictures in the paper, the reading on television? The wonderful reviews? 'This fresh new voice.' I bet you were just scribbling away in notebooks. It wasn't so bad when the odd poem appeared in a small magazine. He probably taunted you that no one but writers and wannabes read them..." I was feeling my way along, thinking that Charlie Trott had humiliated me in just this way. I'd sent poems out, too, and short stories, before writing cookbooks. A waste of postage, Charlie had said. "He probably begrudged you the price of stamps."

"You don't know what you're talking about," Hilary said.

"I think I do. Your husband must be a real psychopath for you to have to hide like this. What I don't understand is why you are playing this charade, hiding your identity from everyone in Meredith. Lots of writers fall on hard times and take odd jobs. I don't understand the secrecy."

"You don't understand anything."

"You could have your husband arrested."

"He's already been in jail. He served two months after he broke my leg. That's why he'll kill me if he finds me."

"Why don't you just forget about writing?" I blurted.

Hilary, caught off guard by the unexpected question, gave me an incredulous look.

"I recognized you tonight, Hilary," I said. "I can't remember your name, but I know your face. I was at my publishers' a few days ago and saw your picture in a book catalogue. Only then you looked like a poet in the picture, and now you look like Hilary, a simple girl who gobbles up romance novels. You shouldn't have looked at the book review paper here."

"You're crazy," Hilary said.

I ignored her. "You had long, frizzy hair in the picture. Hair that hid your sensitive face. The long hair's gone, but the face is the same, Hilary. I bet you've seen that catalogue. On the opposite page is a photo of this man wearing black leather. You were one of the bright, shining lights of the literary world, Hilary. You still are, as far as I am concerned."

"No, you're wrong."

"I'm not wrong. Your work still exists. You're still the same person."

Hilary blushed.

"Well, I do know who you are," I said, "even if I can't recall the name. So why are you hiding out as a writer?"

I think it was the fact that I referred to her as a writer I respected that softened her. For a moment she looked as if she might cry. Here we were, two writers together. We knew that under other circumstances we could sit up all night comparing publishing stories and sharing literary gossip.

How awful it was must have been for her in Meredith, I thought, after the hoopla about her book. I was pretty sure, now, that I'd seen her on television, on a panel show of some sort, as well as in the catalogue. And I'd read a couple of interviews, although I didn't remember the contents. I knew her poems were about women's sexuality.

"You had the answer," Hilary said quietly, and blushed again. She got up to pour more wine and kept her back to me.

"I don't understand."

"You said it."

"What?"

"That writers read those magazines." She whirled around, spilling wine. "Goddamned writers read the goddamned literary magazines! Editors read the damned things! Don't you know how cosy it is in the literary world? Conferences and seminars and meetings— everyone knows someone who knows everyone else!"

"So, what you're telling me is that your husband..."

"... is a writer. And an editor. And a lecturer. And a bloody reviewer! He loves, loves, loves giving advice to young women writers! Mentoring them along!"

Hilary's face was animated. No more Miss Woe Is Me. I could see Hilary, the poet, giving a spirited reading.

"'Come to my study and we'll look at the poems, shall we?'" she mimicked. "'Let's share a loving cup!'" She grimaced and downed the wine. "And you're wrong about the little mags! He was jealous of those, too! He would sulk for days and then he'd fly into a rage over some little thing. He broke an entire set of dishes and a mirror before he broke my leg!"

"He must have been terribly embarrassed about going to jail."

"No one knew. It didn't make the papers and everyone thought he was in Mexico. He was planning to go to Mexico, you see. But they locked him up and I hid out at a second cousin's house and came here after my leg healed. Do you know how he broke my leg? He jumped on it!"

"He jumped on it???"

"He pushed me down a few stairs. He ran up the stairs and jumped! He's a crazy man."

"So... you think if you keep publishing under your old name, he'll find you."

"You got it!"

It was strange to witness the persona of wishy-washy Hilary disappear.

"Gracie found out who you were, didn't she?"

Hilary didn't answer.

"How did Gracie find out?"

"My purse fell open on the floor and she saw *Pride and Prejudice*... I had too much wine to drink and suddenly I felt like a writer again. Before I knew it, I was telling her I'd had a book published. She wanted me to move to Chicago, and I even told her about publishing a poem in a magazine down there!"

"But the next day you realized how foolish you had been. You went to Marion's house to speak to Gracie, to ask her to forget what you'd told her..."

I unplugged the kettle, which was boiling away.

"She even knew my husband's name! You send your mother-in-law your old copies of *Books in Canada*. There was an article in one of them about a husband and wife. Two writers working together, sharing a study. She waved the story in my face! She didn't understand the way the literary community in Canada works."

"She wanted to tell everyone that they had a famous poet in their midst," I surmised. "She really didn't understand that to keep away from your husband, for him never ever to find you, you had to begin again as a writer."

But that wasn't quite it. I was still missing something: the reason Hilary had clunked Gracie on the head. I knew she had done it. Why? Why? Hilary looked not quite smug, but satisfied that I hadn't discovered what Gracie knew.

And in that satisfied look, I could see how Hilary would be, what her image would be: the simple country girl, a writer from the boonies no one had ever heard of. Unlike the poet I had seen in the catalogue, she would not frizz her hair or outline her eyes. She would present her naked face to the world. Being bland, dressed in colourless, even pretty, polyester, her image would be of a talented woman who was totally clueless, unhip, uncool. Later, perhaps, she could alter the image, turn to smart, understated dresses and large hats. But she would never again be that frizzy-haired poet.

Hilary poured more wine.

"I think you have started again," I said. "Some little mag, maybe two little mags, have taken a story, a few poems. You could build on that. But it took a while, didn't it? And you didn't want to invent yourself yet another time, did you?"

I saw from Hilary's face that I was right.

"All that sending out, all those submissions without those nice little letters to the editor saying you've been published in

*Quarry* and the *Fiddlehead*. I know how much easier it is to be published if you've had things published before. So, now you have started again, and you can write, 'Dear Editor, Here is my poem. My work has appeared in...' But Gracie threatened to reveal your new identity. Did she blackmail you?"

"She didn't put it like that. She wanted me to take her to Steven's office so she could steal drugs. I have a key. I clean there twice a week. I wish I'd just given her the key."

"Instead you panicked and hit her? What did you use?"

"A piece of wood from beside the fireplace. It wasn't hard to get rid of. I hid it under my coat and threw it into the woods on my way home."

I moved to the counter and plugged the kettle in again, to get it boiling once more. "Gracie isn't out of the woods yet," I said. Hilary and I might have had many things in common as writers, but Gracie's attempted murder was where we parted company. It was awful, but I was thinking that Hilary would get a lot of publicity from being charged. The story about her husband's abuse would come out, and Hilary would have her supporters, I thought, as the still-hot water came to a roiling boil.

Hilary sprang in front of me.

If she'd had a knife, she might have stuck it in me, but I grabbed her wrist and twisted, hard, just as she reached for the kettle of scalding water.

"You don't want to do that, Hilary."

We stared at each other. In her face I saw the same features that had been hidden by a curtain of frizzy hair. Lucinda— I remembered her first name suddenly, but the last name would not come to me. In another situation we might have met at a reading or launch; I might have bought her book and had it autographed. We would have run into each other at literary functions and conferences. I could see her in de rigueur black, with necklaces and silver rings. "The poet" predicated on one slim volume of poetry, but a slim volume achieved after much striving and effort, hope, and maybe prayer.

"I'm out of here," she whispered. "You'll never see me again."

In a second, she was gone.

## Chapter Eighteen

Lucinda Paradise.

It was probably a pseudonym in the first place. She had grown up in Montreal, I learned. Or at least that was what she had said. Her poetry had been published in the gamut of Canadian literary magazines before her first book came out. She had started reading at festivals around Toronto and a community college in Alberta had invited her for a reading before she disappeared to reinvent herself.

Some might say Lucinda/Hilary took herself too seriously, but these people understand neither the crazy compulsion of the writer to create, nor the difficulty in publishing poetry. Or publishing writing of any kind, for that matter.

And it is not true, exactly, that I let her escape. I did leave the kitchen, and when I returned five minutes later, Hilary, along with her coat and boots, was gone; as was Marion's bug, which was recovered two days later in a mall parking lot in North York. By the time the police had checked Hilary's room at the Meredith Hotel, and while others checked the woods and roads near the lodge for the weapon she'd used on Gracie, Hilary was driving through the night to Toronto. No one noticed Marion's bug missing until much later.

But Lucinda Paradise/Hilary would never be charged with murder. Gracie opened her eyes the following day. She was sitting up when I arrived in the late afternoon. Dazed and disoriented, nauseated, she nevertheless gave me a Gracie-type smile: rueful and amused and totally confident.

"All this because I slipped and banged my head against the table," she said. Her eyelids drooped in a languid way as if she wanted to keep what Hilary had done to her a secret.

Was she being charitable, knowing she had brought much on herself? I told her about contacting Sonia at Mother Line. Gracie neither apologized nor explained, although she did say she hoped Sonia would not fly to Canada as there was no one else she could trust with the business.

"I should not have had so much to drink over Christmas," she said. "And now they tell me I have diabetes. I guess my party days are over, eh? At least for the time being."

I did not mention the morphine and neither did Gracie.

"No wonder I blacked out," Gracie said.

I went out and bought Gracie cosmetics and a bathrobe and nightie because all her things were still in Meredith. "Fool that you are," Allison said to me as she prepared to go home to visit Steven in the Meredith jail. Joe, much relieved that he was "off the hook," would drive her.

"Gracie really says she slipped?" Joe asked. He was much more interested than Allison, who could only think about Steven. "That skinny Hilary didn't hit her?"

"That's what Gracie says."

Joe shook his head, but I think he secretly thought Gracie had had it coming.

"Well, they'll get Hilary for stealing Marion's car, anyway," he said. This was before the car was found. "And I guess Grace will go back where she came from and that will be that."

"I'll have to see her to give her her clothes." And her Christmas presents, I thought. Peter was bringing everything with him when he returned to Guelph with our car.

"You could just dump it off on a desk at the hospital," Joe suggested, but I think he knew I'd speak to Gracie again.

Reg was with Gracie when I delivered her suitcase the next day.

"You two met long ago," was what Gracie said, waving her arm at the small, dapper elderly Romeo with his yellow bow-tie and shiny grey suit who sat by her bed. He was shorter than I remembered, and he had the puffy eyes and bulbous nose of a drinker. I would never have recognized him.

At least this proves this is Gracie and that she really was in Maine, I thought, as I shook Reg's hand.

"Could have knocked me down with a feather when that Sonia said Gracie was in the hospital," Reg said. "You never can tell what goes on in the world, can you? What with one thing and another, terrorists and criminals and children starving..."

He rattled on inconsequentially. He smelled powerfully of after shave and his fingers were stained with nicotine.

"Reg is the custodian at Mother Line," Gracie explained.

She did not explain much else. It was obvious to me as Reg chatted about my grandmother's "home baking" that the others at Mother Line did not know that Reg was Gracie's father, although Reg and Gracie sometimes shared a house that Gracie had bought. But I learned this from Reg, not Gracie. "I still got the tree up for you," is what Reg said, and this led to talk of shovelling the snow and getting a neighbour in to feed the cat.

The house explained a lot: Gracie lived in the apartment hotel under her own name, and in the house under another last name, keeping bank accounts with that address.

"Gracie here has been telling me about the wonderful time you gave her over Christmas," Reg said, "and I want you to know the welcome mat's always out for you and your hubby any time you feel like visiting the Windy City."

"That's right," Gracie echoed. She smiled at me.

I maintained the facade, but wondered if the people at Mother Line would now learn that Reg was Gracie's father.

I doubted it.

Caught in a corner, Gracie's motto appeared to be: never explain.

But her smile was the same and there was no embarrassment when she looked at me. The stories of her "parents" and "Nan" might never have been told.

"Here I am," Gracie seemed to be saying. "Take me as I am."

A dangerous woman, Neil had said. But in that danger was also charity: she was not accusing Hilary of trying to do her in, as if she recognized in Hilary's desperation a reflection of her own need to do whatever she had to do.

I didn't say goodbye to Gracie. She was gone when I turned up at the hospital a few days later.

I've never heard from her since, and I've tried to resist listening to Mother Line. When I finally did, there was Gracie's melodious voice.

No strange packages arrived in our mail. The break-in was

never explained and was probably connected to the other break-ins on our street over the Christmas holidays.

Allison offered to put up bail for Steven, but he would not permit this. He remains in custody, awaiting trail for imposture and practising medicine without a license. Support for him has dwindled in Meredith. There's a new doctor now, a peppy, bright young McMaster grad who has yet to make a house-call.

There was more publicity when the body of *Doctor* Steven MacLeod was found in "the Meredith Steven's" cabin in British Columbia. The doctor's sister was interviewed when she came to Canada. Allison continues to visit her Steven whenever she can.

"Everyone looks at him differently now that they know he's not a doctor," Allison said recently. "But what's wrong with being a male nurse?"

Indeed. Steven's imposture was wrong, and Allison, whose loyalty has surprised me, is right: there is nothing wrong with being a male nurse. But I know what Allison means.

Image, image. We are what we present to the world.

We are not our dreams, our secrecies, our fantasies. Except perhaps to ourselves? Neil continues to bring doughnuts for our chats. We are friends...

And somewhere out there, Hilary, also known as Lucinda Paradise, also known as Whoever, is reinventing herself. Perhaps she's a companion to an elderly woman on the prairies, I imagine, or a waitress in a truckers' diner, but at night she tends the words that will allow her, in time, to blossom once again.